Matters of Coincidence

MATT HAYDOCK

Grosvenor House
Publishing Limited

This book is published by
Grosvenor House Publishing Ltd
Link House
140 The Broadway, Tolworth, Surrey, KT6 7HT.
www.grosvenorhousepublishing.co.uk

This book is a work of fiction. Any resemblance to
people or events, past or present, is purely coincidental.

A CIP record for this book
is available from the British Library

ISBN 978-1-83615-050-3
eBook ISBN 978-1-83615-051-0

To my four wonderful girls:

Alex, Laura, Philippa and Katharine

Preface

Matters of Coincidence is the third book in the **Harfield** trilogy, the first two being **A Work In Progress** and **Think Again!** But there is no need to have read those earlier works in order to enjoy reading this book.

Acknowledgements

I am indebted to those readers of my first two novels in this series who provided feedback and helpful criticism.

In particular, I want to express my deep gratitude to my wife, Alex, without whose patience, constant encouragement and support, none of the books in this trilogy would ever have seen the light of day. And, Oh! What a loss to mankind that would have been.

Alex also created the cover of this book, just like she did for the other two.

DAY ONE – TUESDAY

It wasn't supposed to end like this. But actions have consequences that are sometimes unforeseen and unwelcome. This was one of those occasions. And it left Charlie Rich anxious and confused. Why didn't the man just let go of his briefcase? If he hadn't struggled so hard to keep it, he wouldn't have slipped and hit his head on the kerb. And he wouldn't now be..........

Charlie knelt down to take a closer look. The man wasn't moving and there was blood, lots of blood. But he might not be dead. If he was, then Charlie knew it was manslaughter and that could mean life. At the very least it meant a long stretch inside, especially for someone with his criminal record.

People were now beginning to appear. A couple with a dog were less than a hundred yards away and approaching fast. At any moment they would see the man's body lying on the ground. And then what? Charlie knew he had to leave, and quickly. Taking hold of his victim's briefcase, he stood up and started to run. Still conflicted, he promised himself he would ring for an ambulance, just as soon as he was away and safe.

But he never did.

DAY TWO – WEDNESDAY

At Oxford Police HQ, Detective Inspector Janet Kershaw was just finishing off her umpteenth coffee of the morning. She needed the caffeine. It had been a long night with very little opportunity for sleep. And it wasn't over yet. There were still a few things left to do, and the clock on her office wall said it was already 11.00 am. She needed to get a move on.

The bag-snatch killing was the most serious crime DI Kershaw had investigated since her recent promotion. And, as a young and ambitious police officer, she was understandably keen to demonstrate her competence by getting it wrapped up quickly.

Although ideally, she would have preferred a case that was, perhaps, a little more complex and challenging, one in which she could really demonstrate her capabilities as a detective, at least she'd got this one solved. She'd identified the killer and gathered an impressive mass of evidence to prove it.

All that remained, apart from the inevitable paperwork, of course, was to make the arrest. And DI Kershaw was preparing to do just that, when her boss, Chief Superintendent David Evans, unexpectedly entered her office. He was accompanied by a second, much taller, man.

"This is Superintendent Ifor Jenkins," Evans explained. "He's come from the Met to offer his assistance with your investigation. You'll probably recognise him as the officer who played a central role in the recent Gant case."

Assistance! I don't need any bloody assistance, thought Kershaw. Visibly vexed at Evans's suggestion, that she might, she responded with a note of sarcasm. "How could I possibly fail to recognise the Superintendent, Sir? His face was all over the newspapers and TV for the best part of a fortnight. Involvement in the Gant case has made him into something of a celebrity."

Kershaw dropped her fake smile, only to replace it with an equally false look of serious concern, before turning to look Jenkins square in the face and ratchetting up the sarcasm another notch. "But you must have been very disappointed when you lost Gant before he got to trial. Shot by an unknown assassin, I seem to remember. It didn't end well. Did it, Sir?"

"No, you're right, it didn't end well," Jenkins responded coolly. "Either for Gant or, the criminal organisation he'd been a member of. The one we completely dismantled."

Chief Superintendent Evans, never the most self confident and assertive of senior police officers, reacted to the less than warm and welcoming atmosphere by moving towards the door. "I'll leave you to brief Superintendent Jenkins, Inspector Kershaw. Just keep me informed of progress....... and let me know if you need anything." And, with only a faint smile in the direction of Jenkins, Evans was gone.

"Well, I'm very grateful for your generous offer of help, Sir," said Kershaw, the sarcasm in her tone still palpable, "but it doesn't look like I'll be in need of it. If the Chief

Super hadn't left quite so hurriedly, I'd have told him I've already identified the killer. He's a low-life addict and minor drug dealer called Charlie Rich. Although he's never been known to commit a street robbery before and has no history of violence, the evidence against him is pretty overwhelming. Half a dozen people have identified him as the person they saw running away from the scene, with what we have reason to believe was the victim's briefcase. And we've also got him on at least half a dozen CCTV cameras. Very helpfully, he even left his bloodied handprints in several places, on and around the body. He's got a criminal record that stretches back years, but until now he's mainly restricted himself to low level drug dealing and opportunistic thieving and burglary. He's been in and out of jail ever since he was a teenager, but he'll stay in for a lot longer this time. Causing death during the commission of a robbery, even without intent, means he's going to be charged with manslaughter. I've just finished reading the pathologist's report on the victim. The cause of death was severe trauma to the brain."

"So you see it as just some petty career criminal branching out with a random bag snatch that's gone wrong? And nothing more?" said Jenkins.

Kershaw was puzzled by Jenkins' apparent scepticism. "Sure, open and shut, I'd say. If the victim hadn't hit his head on the kerb, Charlie would be looking at doing no more than two years, even with his record. As it now stands, he'll be lucky to be out in ten. I was just about to get my team together and go round to his place and arrest him."

"Would you mind if I come along?" asked Jenkins.

Kershaw gave a shrug. "Sure, by all means, Sir."

Charlie Rich's home was a third floor studio flat in a low rise block, located in what is just about the least salubrious district that Oxford has to offer. Kershaw and her crew had brought along a door ram, but they needn't have bothered. Just before they smashed their way in, Jenkins stepped forward and opened the door with nothing more than a turn of the handle and a gentle push.

The officers rushed in, yelling out that they were the police and that everyone should stay where they were. But there was absolutely no need. Seated in an armchair, naked, except for a grubby pair of underpants and a single sock dangling off the end of his left foot, Charlie Rich was alone and going nowhere.

There was a single bullet hole in the left side of his chest and another in his forehead. White powder was splattered all around his open mouth. A large cream coloured envelope, stuffed with twenty pound notes, lay on the floor by his side, its position suggesting it had fallen out of his dead right hand.

An open and empty briefcase was standing on the table. Although somewhat faded with age, the victim's initials were still just about visible in black lettering on its side, confirming it was the one Charlie had stolen the previous evening. The remains of its broken lock and a rusty pair of pliers were lying alongside. It had obviously been forced open.

Charlie's flat was a shambolic stinking dump, with a colour scheme best described as a dismal shade of drab.

But, despite this egregious state, there was nothing to suggest that any kind of struggle had taken place. Concluding that the killer must have had Charlie's compliance from beginning to end, Jenkins turned his attention to the body.

Two bullets had passed straight through Charlie and then through the armchair he was sitting in. Jenkins pointed out to Kershaw where they must have ended up, lodged in the wall behind. But they weren't there anymore. Someone had gone to the trouble of removing them.

"This shows all the signs of having been a professional hit," said Jenkins. "Do you still think what happened yesterday was a random bag snatch gone wrong?"

Kershaw's antagonism had evaporated and all she could do was slowly shake her head. For the moment, she didn't know what to think. Until the discovery of Charlie Rich's murdered body, she had simply assumed that his bag-snatch victim was just some poor unfortunate, who happened to be in the wrong place at the wrong time. Merely someone who was randomly and opportunistically selected to be robbed, for no better reason than because he was carrying a briefcase that might contain something of value. But now she wasn't quite so sure.

Charlie Rich existed in a world of drugs and criminality, a world fraught with insecurity and violence. It was certainly possible, perhaps even likely, that his murder was totally unrelated to the street robbery he'd carried out the previous evening, but the possibility of a connection had to be considered.

After calling in a forensics team to examine the murder scene and sending members of her own crew to carry out neighbourhood enquiries, DI Kershaw returned to Oxford Police HQ. Jenkins went with her. There was no longer a suspect to arrest, but there was now even more paperwork to complete and a new case to begin work on, the cold blooded murder of Charlie Rich.

"Other than the briefcase, do you know if Charlie Rich took anything else from his victim?" Jenkins asked.

DI Kershaw emptied out the contents of a large envelope onto her desk. "I can't say for certain, but it doesn't look like it. This is what the victim still had on him when he was found. If Charlie did take anything else, then you'd think he would have taken some of this stuff as well?"

Jenkins examined each of the various items in turn: an expensive looking gold watch; a mobile phone; a leather wallet, containing bank cards and over a hundred pounds in cash; a gold pen; a bunch of keys; and, finally, a small pocket notebook.

Jenkins was surprised at what Charlie Rich had left behind. "Once his victim was incapacitated, he could have taken any of this stuff without a problem," he said. "So, why didn't he?"

"He probably panicked and was in a rush to get away, when he realised his victim was seriously hurt," suggested Kershaw. "Like I told you earlier, Sir, Charlie has no previous history of violence."

Jenkins wasn't convinced. "Maybe you're right, but it didn't stop him running away with the briefcase, did it? Why would he do that? Why would he carry home, something that could so clearly connect him to a very serious crime, yet still leave all this other stuff behind?"

"I don't know, Sir," Kershaw replied, "but he must have been very disappointed when he got home and discovered the briefcase was empty."

"What makes you think that?" asked Jenkins. "Just because it was empty when we found it, doesn't mean it was empty when Charlie Rich stole it. Its contents could have been taken away by his killer."

The pocket notebook was the last item Jenkins picked up from the desk. Containing barely a dozen entries of names, addresses and telephone numbers, it didn't take long for him to quickly thumb his way through its pages, pausing for a few moments on just one of them.

When he'd finished, he placed the notebook back on the desk and immediately looked at his watch. "I have a personal matter to attend to and it might take a while," he said. "I'll catch up with you later." Before Kershaw had an opportunity to ask any questions, he was gone.

After leaving Oxford Police HQ, Jenkins drove the fifteen miles to the ancient village of Prinsted, to the home of former army major turned priest, The Reverend Chris Brazelle. The two men had first become acquainted with one another during their mutual involvement in the Gant case. It was an affair in which Brazelle had, in fact, played a pivotal role, although only a handful of people, in addition to Jenkins, were aware of this. And Brazelle had his reasons for wanting it to remain like that.

Jenkins had given no prior warning of his visit but fortunately Brazelle was at home when he arrived.

"This isn't exactly a social call, Chris," explained Jenkins. "I'm afraid I've come as the bearer of some bad news. Later today, the identity of the man who was killed in a street robbery in Oxford last night will be released to the media. His name is Graham Davey. He was Professor of History at Oxford University, and I believe you may have known him."

Brazelle was clearly taken by surprise. "I'm very sorry to hear that. I heard about the robbery on the news, of course, but I had no idea the victim was Professor Davey. And you're right, I did know him, although only very slightly. How did you get to know that?"

"He had a pocket notebook on him when he was killed and it has your name and phone number written in it," replied Jenkins. "I'm curious to know why."

"Well, I'll be happy to satisfy your curiosity," responded Brazelle. "But I'm a little curious about something myself. I'm pretty sure Oxford comes under Thames Valley Police. How come a Superintendent from the Met is involved in investigating a crime that took place within their jurisdiction?"

"I'm afraid that's not a question I'm able to answer, at least not just yet," replied Jenkins. "In fact I'm not even certain I know the true reason myself. But there are a few things I can tell you. It's all stuff that hasn't been made public yet, although it will be very soon. For a start, Davey's death was almost certainly unintended. He was robbed by a petty criminal with no history of violence, a well known local drug addict and low level dealer called Charlie Rich. And he's also now dead. We found his body at his home a couple of hours ago. He'd been shot twice and it shows all the signs of having been a cold blooded professional execution. One that took place very soon after Charlie returned home with the Professor's stolen briefcase. It's possible that the robbery of Professor Davey and the murder of Charlie Rich are completely unrelated, of course, but it's too soon to draw a conclusion, either one way or the other. Before I can do that, I'll need to learn a lot more about Professor Davey. Perhaps I'll come up with a reason why there might be a link between the two crimes. That's why I'm here. I thought I might as well start by finding out how you and Davey came to be connected."

"Well, to tell the truth it wasn't much of a connection at all. In fact I hardly knew the man," explained Brazelle. "I met him for the first time just six weeks ago, when I went to consult him on a matter concerning the history of the Harfield family. It turned out to be something that took his interest and he decided to spend some time researching the subject. The next time we met was here in Prinsted, about a week later, when he came to give me an update on the progress of his research. That was the last time we had any contact, until he unexpectedly phoned three days ago. But it was only a very brief call. He said he'd located a document that should prove useful in his Harfield research and that he'd let me have more details very soon. That was all. Before I could ask him any questions he'd hung up."

Jenkins seriously doubted that the history of the Harfield family could have any bearing on the case he was investigating, but he was still curious to know what had prompted Brazelle to consult Professor Davey about it.

Brazelle showed Jenkins the photograph of a young woman's portrait. "I wanted to talk to him about the woman in this picture. Her name is Adeline. She was the wife of Sir Richard, the First Baronet Harfield. The couple were the first Harfields to set up home in Prinsted, after moving here from London in 1685. They were the people who built the original Harfield House, at the northern edge of the village, although few traces of it remain. It was demolished by their great grandson almost a century later, and then replaced with the four-storey Georgian mansion that stands there today."

Brazelle was well acquainted with the history of the Harfield family and their ancestral residence, Harfield House. It was the home of his fiancée, Rose Harfield. She shared the property with her much older half-sister, Lady Frances Marshall, and her husband, Sir Damien Marshall, a senior British diplomat.

The two Harfield sisters had inherited joint ownership of the entire Harfield Estate, following the murder of their father, Sir Cornelius, the Eleventh Baronet Harfield, just over twenty years earlier. However, they had only recently returned to live in the Georgian mansion, having been resident in America during the two decades since their father's death.

Sir Cornelius had been married twice. Frances was the daughter of his first wife, Brigitte, whilst Rose was the daughter of his second wife, Justine. Both of his wives had predeceased him.

Ever since the time of Sir Richard and Lady Adeline, the Harfield family had been major land and property owners in and around Prinsted. Even Brazelle's current home, Holford's Cottage, belonged to the Harfield Estate. Brazelle was renting the property, whilst acting as locum Prinsted parish priest. He was temporarily covering for the permanent incumbent, The Reverend Jenny Caulfield, whilst she was on maternity-leave, expecting her first child.

Jenkins had visited Harfield House on a few occasions and was acquainted with both Harfield sisters, but he knew very little about their family's history. What he'd just been told made him curious to know what was so special about Lady Adeline that Brazelle had decided to consult Professor Davey about her.

"It was because of who she allegedly claimed to be," Brazelle explained. "According to an entry in one of her great grandson's journals, she claimed to be the only legitimate child of King Charles II, and therefore, after his death, the rightful Queen of England. Professor Davey was an expert on that particular period in British history. That's why I went to see him. I thought he'd immediately give me a hundred reasons why the claim had to be most certainly false. As it turned out, he couldn't come up with a single one. In fact he gave me an even bigger surprise by saying he'd like to research the possibility that it might actually be true. He said there's a six month period during King Charles' enforced exile abroad that's never been properly explained, or accounted for. Apparently, the details of Adeline's claim fitted right into it."

Jenkins appeared somewhat sceptical, to say the least. "Well, that's all news to me," he said. "I studied the Tudors and Stuarts for A Level History, but I certainly don't remember being told anything like that."

"I'd be very surprised if you had been," said Brazelle. "It's probably one of British history's best kept secrets."

"You're beginning to sound like it's something you believe. Do you?" asked Jenkins.

"I certainly wouldn't say that I was entirely convinced," replied Brazelle. "But I'm certainly leaning that way. And so was Professor Davey. At first he was extremely sceptical, just as I was, and just as you appear to be now. But after considering all the evidence that seemed to support the claim, we both came to believe that it was, at the very least, plausible and might very well be true."

Jenkins had learnt from first-hand experience that Brazelle was a sophisticated and analytical thinker, and certainly not someone who could be easily duped into falling for a hoax. And, if Graham Davey, an eminent Professor of History, had also come to believe that Adeline's alleged claim might possibly be true then, surely, he thought, there must be some pretty convincing evidence to support it. Although still sceptical, he found himself sufficiently intrigued to want to learn more.

Brazelle was happy to oblige.............

The story began with the discovery of Adeline's portrait. It had been found hidden away in the basement of Harfield House, less than two months earlier. It was more or less stumbled upon by Frances Marshall and the housekeeper, Megan Richards, whilst they were sorting through a numerous and varied collection of paintings, artefacts and general detritus, that had been allowed to accumulate in the basement over many years.

When first discovered, the portrait was very much a mystery. Nobody in the household admitted to having prior knowledge even of its existence. And it was several days before its subject was finally identified as Lady Adeline, with any degree of certainty.

According to what was written in the bottom right hand corner of the portrait, it had been painted by Sir Godfrey Kneller, who at the time was Principal Painter in Ordinary to the English Royal Court, shortly before Adeline and Sir Richard were married in 1681.

Keen to verify the painting's authenticity as a genuine Kneller, Frances Marshall arranged for it to be appraised by Professor John Simms, the country's foremost expert on Kneller's work.

After carrying out an extensive examination of the portrait, privately, Simms was happy to confirm that it was a genuine Kneller and, indeed, an excellent exemplar of the artist's work. However, due to the presence of certain symbols and images that appeared in the painting, he refused to declare his opinion publicly.

Simms was confident he could explain the meaning of the mystifying features when considering them individually. But when they were interpreted collectively, as they had to be, they created a narrative he found utterly baffling. What they suggested, Professor Simms asserted, was that the woman was a literate, French speaking unmarried virgin, and a devout Catholic. And he considered that particular part of the narrative to be straightforward. What he found perplexing, was that the woman was also portrayed as enjoying a very special and uniquely close relationship with

King Charles II, although she was certainly not one of his many mistresses or numerous illegitimate offspring.

One feature Simms found particularly puzzling, was the appearance in the painting's background of a miniature portrait of King Charles II, a small scale reproduction of one that Kneller himself had painted a few years earlier. It was something that could never have appeared in Adeline's portrait without the King's clearly expressed permission – an extraordinary privilege that was never granted to anyone else.

Also adding to the mystery, was the fact that Adeline had been painted wearing rubies that Simms identified as having once belonged to King Charles II's mother, Queen Henrietta Maria. It was jewellery which the Queen was known to have given to her son during his forced exile, when Oliver Cromwell held power. In his lifetime, Charles never explained what he did with his mother's gift. And it was generally thought to have been either lost or sold, a presumption that had persisted until the present day. For Simms, none of this made any sense.

Before the discovery of Lady Adeline's portrait, neither Brazelle nor either of the two Harfield sisters knew very much about her. All they knew for sure was what was written on her headstone in the graveyard, such as her dates of birth and death, information that confirmed she had survived well into her nineties. There was also a short Bible inscription written in French. Its appearance on her headstone suggested that Adeline herself may have been French, but that was far from certain.

From the little that Brazelle did know about Adeline, it was clear that she had lived long enough to see her great grandson, Sir Bernard, Fourth Baronet Harfield, reach his mid twenties. He was the person who, in the late eighteenth century, had the original Harfield House demolished and replaced with the Georgian mansion. Once the rebuild was complete, all that remained of the original Harfield House was part of its basement, preserved under the southwest corner of the new building. And it was only very recently that Brazelle had come to understand why it had been retained, when all other traces of the earlier mansion had been demolished. Hidden behind one of its wall panels he'd discovered the entrance to an underground tunnel.

The tunnel stretched for almost two hundred yards, before reaching its exit, which was concealed in an outbuilding in a thickly wooded area, well away from the House. Brazelle reasoned that it must have been created as an emergency escape route out of the House. It seemed to be the only logical explanation for the tunnel's existence. But why, he wondered, had it been thought to be needed?

A portrait of Sir Bernard was hanging in the library of Harfield House. It showed him sitting at a desk, holding a quill pen in his right hand, whilst, with his left hand, opening a book with the word 'Journal' written on its front cover in gold letters. He was clearly being portrayed as a keen diarist and chronicler, someone who kept a written record of the major events in his life.

Brazelle was familiar with all of the portraits that hung in the library of Harfield House, including that of Sir Bernard. After the discovery of Adeline's portrait, he began to consider the possibility that Sir Bernard might have made a written record, not just of the major events of his own life, but also of some of his great grandmother's. After all, their lives had overlapped by more than two decades, giving Adeline plenty of time to pass on all kinds of information, some of which might help to explain the enigmatic symbols and images that appeared in her portrait.

But first, assuming they still existed, Sir Bernard's Journals had to be found. Despite no one in the Harfield household claiming to know anything about them, Brazelle was optimistic that they might still exist. What he had learnt about the generations of wealthy Harfields, led him to believe that they were highly unlikely to have disposed of such a collection of family heirlooms. On the other hand, having also learnt how secretive the family could be, he was quite prepared to believe that the journals might have been hidden away somewhere.

Frances Marshall certainly didn't know where Sir Bernard's journals were. All she could confirm for sure was that they were not in the basement that she'd so recently been clearing. And neither were they in the library. As far as she was concerned, if they did still exist and were going to be found anywhere, then it was almost certainly going to be somewhere in her late father's studio, on the top floor of the House. And she gave Brazelle permission to go there and search for them.

Sir Cornelius's studio also seemed to Brazelle to be the most logical place to begin his search. For one thing, it was the only room in the entire property that had been left exactly as it was on the day Sir Cornelius died, more than twenty years earlier. But that certainly wasn't the only reason.

The desk at which Sir Bernard had been shown sitting in his portrait was the same one that Sir Cornelius, many years later, used himself. And it was still there, in his studio, untouched since the day of his death.

The desk was a work of true craftsmanship, displaying a fusion of two characteristic styles: Chippendale and Chinese Qing dynasty. At the time it was made, in the mid-to-late eighteenth century, it would not have been unusual to find such a grand item of furniture in the home of a wealthy English gentleman.

Although certainly no expert on antique furniture, Brazelle was still aware of the effect that an oriental influence might have had, on the less obvious aspects of the desk's construction. For one thing, he knew that it was quite common for Chinese furniture makers to include hidden compartments in their creations, especially cabinets and desks. With that thought in mind, he began by searching through the desk's drawers. None contained anything of great interest, but one turned out to be quite a bit shorter than the other five.

During his days in the military, Brazelle had often gone in search of things that people didn't want him to find. And these numerous episodes had led him to construct a useful rule-of-thumb: always start with the odd one out. So he did.

The short drawer could not be pulled straight out but, through probing with his fingers, Brazelle eventually located a small release-catch that enabled him to extract it. In the previously hidden space behind, he found three books, each labelled 'Journal' in gold lettering. There was also an envelope addressed to Sir Cornelius, which Brazelle took to be evidence that the 11th Baronet Harfield must have known of the journals' existence. Perhaps he was even the person who placed them in the hidden compartment.

A cursory flick through the pages of the journals quickly confirmed they were the ones kept by Sir Bernard and contained an autobiographical record of events in his life. Each volume covered a period of several years.

On the first page of the earliest of the three volumes there was a dedication stating that it had been given to Sir Bernard, on 17th July, 1756, as a twenty-first birthday gift from his great grandmother, Adeline. It appeared that Sir Bernard's career as a diarist and chronicler had begun when he received his great grandmother's gift and, judging by the date of the last entry in the third volume, ended shortly before his death.

Having confirmed that the journals were the ones he had been looking for, Brazelle focussed on those pages that covered the period when Adeline was still alive. Most of the entries were relatively brief and there were frequent and, sometimes, quite lengthy gaps between them. Fascinating though these passages may have been, Brazelle chose not to spend time reading all the way through them, but continued turning pages, until he eventually discovered what he had been hoping to find.

Sir Bernard had made a record of what he claimed to be a memoir, dictated to him by his great grandmother, Lady Adeline, shortly before her death. Brazelle could scarcely believe what he was reading. Not only did it explain the presence of the symbols and images in Adeline's enigmatic portrait, and account for how she came to be painted wearing Queen Henrietta Maria's rubies, it also appeared to solve a number of other Harfield family mysteries. Not least of which were the original source of the family's considerable wealth and why Prinsted had been chosen as the place for the family to settle in.

According to what was written, Adeline was born in December 1659, in Bollezeele, a large and fairly prosperous village in north east France. Her mother was a member of the de la Valleé family, minor gentry, who, at one time had been the most affluent family in the village. A short while before Adeline's birth, however, due to some poor investment decisions that were made by her maternal grandfather, the family had fallen on relatively hard times. It was during that period when King Charles arrived at the family home, a fugitive seeking a place of shelter, somewhere to hide from Cromwell's spies and would-be assassins.

The story related how the King fell in love with Adeline's mother and married her in a secret ceremony in the village's Catholic Church. Apart from the bride, the groom, and the officiating priest, the only other people present at the ceremony were: the bride's parents; the King's private secretary, Monsieur Allard; and, commander of the King's bodyguard, Colonel John Aston.

A few months after the marriage, it was considered safe enough for Charles to come out of hiding, but his wife, who was by then pregnant with Adeline, remained with her parents at the de la Valleé family home in Bollezeele.

Adeline was born six months later but, sadly, just a few days after the birth, her mother died. At the time, Charles was still not restored to the throne, so he decided it would be best to leave his new born daughter in Bollezeele, in the care of her maternal grandparents, at least for a little while longer.

As it turned out, Adeline remained living with her grandparents for the next twenty years. It was only after both of them had died that King Charles eventually had Adeline brought to England, although her true identity continued to be a closely guarded secret, one that was kept even from Adeline herself. It wasn't until the King was on his deathbed that he finally revealed the truth to her. By then, she was already married and had a young son, also named Charles.

Adeline's husband, Sir Richard, was a man who had risen from poverty and obscurity, to be commander of the King's Guards Regiment and one of the King's most trusted confidantes. The King had informed Richard of Adeline's true identity, shortly before the couple were married, but had made him promise never to reveal it to anyone else, not even to Adeline herself.

In his deathbed confession to Adeline, King Charles explained why he had kept her true identity such a closely guarded secret and why she would be well advised to maintain that secrecy. Adeline had been born to a French mother who was both a commoner and a devout Catholic. And Adeline herself was also a French born woman who was passionate about her Catholic faith. These were all factors, the King asserted, that would make it impossible for her to ever sit securely on the Throne of England. He had, he insisted, kept the truth of her identity from her and from the rest of the world, in order to protect her.

"If your true identity were ever to become generally known, there will be few who wish you well," the King reportedly told Adeline. "But there will be many who wish you ill."

The memoir also claimed that it was King Charles who had commissioned Sir Godfrey Kneller to paint Adeline's portrait. And he had instructed a mystified, yet obedient, Kneller to incorporate the miniature painting of himself in the portrait's background. It was also at the King's request, expressed via Richard Harfield, that Adeline wore the rubies, at one time the property of his mother, whilst she sat for Sir Godfrey. Once completed, the King had the portrait hung in his bedchamber, where he would see it every day.

Charles had given his mother's rubies to Adeline when she became engaged to Sir Richard. At the time, still unaware that she was his daughter, Adeline assumed that the King had presented her with such a beautiful and valuable engagement gift, solely because he was her fiancé's extremely generous employer.

Adeline's memoir also identified the hitherto unknown source of her and her husband's considerable wealth. When he was on his deathbed, King Charles granted to Sir Richard a generous pension and gratuity, in gratitude for his many years of loyal service. It was indeed a most handsome award that Sir Richard received, but it was dwarfed by a far more substantial bequest that the King made to Adeline in his Will.

Details of Adeline's inheritance, however, did not appear in the main body of the King's Will, which inevitably became a public document, but in an appended Codicil, which remained strictly private. Only the King's two executors, Monsieur Allard and Colonel Aston, would know the contents of the Codicil and, apart from Adeline and Sir Richard, no one else was to be made aware even of its existence.

And there was one final puzzle that was solved by Adeline's recorded memoir. It was the mystery of how Sir Richard had risen from the most humble of origins, to become Commander of the King's Guards Regiment and one of King Charles' most trusted aides.

According to the journal's narrative, Richard met King Charles for the first time on Tuesday 12th June, 1660. It was also the day on which he assumed the name Richard Harfield for the first time, his original name being Adam Wellings. At the time, he was a penniless nineteen year old orphan and a falsely accused fugitive from the Law, living in near destitution on the streets of London.

On that particular day, Richard had been just one spectator amongst many, as the King's coach passed by. However, when three would-be regicidal assassins attacked the King's carriage, Richard was the only one to remain calm and bravely eliminate the threat, thereby saving the King's life.

A grateful monarch immediately offered his young saviour a position in the King's Guards regiment, the military unit that formed his personal bodyguard. It was an offer very readily accepted. And for the next twenty years Richard gave loyal service to the King, rising steadily through the ranks until, following the retirement of Colonel Aston in 1680, he became the Regiment's Colonel and Commanding Officer.

As one further mark of distinction, shortly before Richard's marriage to Adeline, King Charles conferred upon him the hereditary title of baronet, making him Sir Richard, First Baronet Harfield.

King Charles had given orders that, upon his death, Sir Richard should immediately resign his commission and leave London with his family, taking Adeline's portrait with him. On the day the King died, Richard carried out those instructions and chose Prinsted, a village some seventy miles north of London, as the place to make his new home.

Prinsted was a village Sir Richard knew well. It was where, in 1642, he had been born to William and Mary Wellings and christened with the name Adam. Then, when both his parents died of the fever, just a few short months after his birth, he had been adopted by the elderly village priest, The Reverend Richard Shuttleworth. And sixteen years later, soon after the death of his adoptive father, it was the place from where he was forced to flee for his life, after being falsely accused of stealing church silver, by The Reverend Shuttleworth's successor as Prinsted parish priest, The Reverend Ambrose Snook, and his wife, Chastity Snook.

Having finished telling Jenkins everything that he had previously told Professor Davey, Brazelle paused, keen to know what Jenkins was thinking. "Given everything you've just heard, do you feel that Adeline's alleged claim has the ring of truth?" he asked.

"Well it's quite a tale," replied Jenkins, "I'll give you that. And I can certainly see why Professor Davey might have found it interesting. But I can't see how he would have been convinced by it."

"At that stage, he wasn't," said Brazelle. "It wasn't until later he considered that the probability had shifted significantly in favour of the claim being true."

Brazelle went on to explain that very soon after their first meeting, Professor Davey had travelled to France, in search of the relevant church records. He believed that the Catholic priest who was in office in Bollezeele at the time of King Charles' sojourn there, was almost certain to have made a parish register entry recording the marriage between Charles and Adeline's mother, regardless of the ceremony having been held in secret. Davey was also convinced that the christening of Adeline and the death and burial of her mother would also have been documented within the parish records. Assuming the events actually took place, of course.

"The Catholic Church is a bureaucratic organisation and always has been," Davey had told Brazelle. "Any act carried out by one of its priests on behalf of the Church has always had to be documented. Even the ones carried out in secret. It's just a question of whether those particular records still exist and can be found."

"And did he find them?" asked Jenkins.

"Not exactly," Brazelle replied. "And oddly enough that was one of the reasons he came eventually to believe that the story might very likely be true."

Brazelle explained that Professor Davey had located the Bollezeele parish records for the year 1659 stored in the Archives of the Catholic Diocesan office in St Omer. According to the Archives' own records, they had been deposited there in March 1688, shortly after the death of Father Levesque, who'd been the parish priest in Bollezeele for the previous thirty years.

The records covering the period of Levesque's incumbency were written in a collection of three volumes, with a page devoted to each of its three hundred and sixty months. Having inspected those volumes, Davey had told Brazelle that Levesque appeared to have been a model bureaucrat, and that his calligraphy and attention to detail in his record keeping were excellent. There was just one problem – not all of the three hundred and sixty pages were present. Just two pages, those detailing the months of March and December of 1659, appeared to have been very carefully removed.

It was in March 1659 that Adeline claimed her parents were married. And it was in December of the same year that Adeline was born and christened, and when her mother died and was buried. The absence of the records for those two particular months was hard to fathom. Was it just pure coincidence? It was certainly something that the Diocesan Archivist couldn't explain. She insisted that the care and security of the parish registers, and all the other documents stored within the Archives, had always been given the highest priority. Perhaps someone had removed the missing pages before the Bollezeele Parish Registers were ever deposited in the Archives, she suggested. Maybe Father Levesque himself had been responsible for their removal. But the Archivist was at a loss to explain why he, or anyone else for that matter, would have wanted to do that.

"Does any of this make you feel less sceptical about Adeline's alleged claim, like it did Professor Davey?" Brazelle asked.

"Well, if it is a hoax, it seems that someone's gone to a lot of trouble to carry it out," said Jenkins. "Who else knows what you've just told me?"

"A very good question," replied Brazelle. "Ever since its discovery, Adeline's portrait has been hanging in the library at Harfield House, so quite a few people will have seen it and know that she was the wife of Sir Richard, First Baronet Harfield. But, as far as I'm aware, I am the only person left alive who's read the first of Sir Bernard's three journals. That means the only people who I'm sure know the whole story, including details of Adeline's claim to a royal heritage, are those I've told myself. With Professor Davey now dead, that just leaves you and Gerald Caulfield."

Jenkins was not surprised to hear that Brazelle had told Dr Gerald Caulfield, the Prinsted village doctor and husband of The Reverend Jenny Caulfield. He knew he was probably Brazelle's closest friend. But what about the two Harfield sisters? Hadn't Brazelle told them?

"So far I haven't told either Frances or Rose anything about Adeline's alleged memoir," confirmed Brazelle. "They don't even know that Sir Bernard wrote in three journals. I've only given them his second and third volumes to read, and he only wrote in those a long time after Adeline's death. They don't even mention her name, let alone have anything to say about her alleged claim. I know it will probably strike you as surprising that I haven't told them, especially given what it would appear to mean for each of them, personally, assuming it all turns out to be true. But, for reasons I'm not going into right now, telling them won't be as straightforward a matter as you might think. Before I even contemplate doing that, I'll need to be totally convinced of the truth of Adeline's alleged claim myself. Otherwise, and please trust me on this, I might be stirring up a hornet's nest for no good reason."

Jenkins looked at his watch. His visit to Prinsted had taken up far more time than he'd anticipated. "It's certainly a fascinating story," he said. "But right now I'm involved in a murder investigation and I'd better get back to focussing on that. I can't see how there might be a connection between what you've just told me and what happened to Davey but, if something turns up that causes me to change my mind about that, I'll make sure you're one of the first people to know about it. In the meantime I'll keep what you've just told me to myself."

On his return to Oxford Police HQ Jenkins went straight to Kershaw's office. He was eager to catch up with developments.

"I'm afraid I can't tell you what's been happening," explained a despondent sounding DI Kershaw. "Soon after you left I was taken off the case. Charlie Rich was a known dealer and his murder shows all the signs of being a professional hit. So the Chief reckons it's almost certainly drugs related and completely unconnected to last night's bag snatch. And he appears to have decided that makes it far too big a case for little-old-me to handle. So he's passed it over to the Serious Crime Squad."

"And it's pretty clear to see you're disappointed with that decision," observed Jenkins.

"Of course I am," Kershaw responded abruptly. "I thought this might be the case where I'd be able to demonstrate my full potential as a detective and give my career a well-needed boost into the bargain. I would have thought that you, of all people, would understand. I heard you moved up two ranks in just four months, and all because of your involvement in the Gant case."

It suddenly dawned on Kershaw that she was almost certainly overstepping the mark in the way she was speaking to a more senior officer. She quickly apologised. "Sorry, Sir, that was totally out of order, I didn't mean to make it personal."

Jenkins did indeed understand. He'd experienced such disappointments once or twice in his own career. "I'll let it pass.......this time," he said, with a gentle nod of forgiveness.

"I'm also sorry we got off on the wrong foot earlier, Sir," said Kershaw, "and it was entirely my fault. My behaviour was extremely unprofessional. I know it's no excuse, but I got very little sleep last night and when you arrived out of the blue like that, I thought you might try and take over the case. But it now seems I had the wrong suspect. Ever since I was a kid, all I ever wanted to do was join the police and become a detective. On days like this, though, I wonder if I made the right career choice. Was it like that for you, Sir?"

Jenkins shook his head. "No, I don't remember ever giving a thought to having a career in the police. I studied Law at university and, a couple of months before graduation, my tutor said he could arrange an introduction to one of the country's biggest law firms. It was only when I turned up for the interview that I found out he meant the Metropolitan Police Service. And it's been all hearts and flowers ever since."

For the first time since Jenkins met Kershaw he saw her smile. "Is any of that actually true?" she asked.

Jenkins returned the smile. "Just the bit about me studying Law."

Kershaw looked at her watch. "Well, I'm off the case and, as of five minutes ago, I'm also off duty. Can I apologise for my behaviour by buying you a drink, Sir?"

"Yes you certainly can. I could do with a drink," replied Jenkins, "But first, if you could just hang on a couple of minutes, I need to make a very brief phone-call."

The Celestial Gardens Chinese Bar and Restaurant is tucked away in one of the many ancient side streets in central Oxford. Jenkins took the bar stool next to Kershaw and looked around to appreciate the colourful and classically oriental décor. "When you invited me to have a drink, this isn't quite what I was expecting," he said. "Are you a regular here?"

"I wouldn't exactly call myself a regular," replied Kershaw, "but I do come here from time to time. A couple of years ago I went on a month long tour of China and acquired a taste for Chinese booze. This is just about the only place around here where they serve it. But they stock the local stuff as well."

From where Jenkins was sitting he had a view right through the bar and into the separate restaurant area. Even though it was still relatively early on a midweek evening he could see that the place was already more than half full. And he noticed that most of the clientele appeared to be young ethnic Chinese.

"It's very popular with the Chinese students at the University," explained Kershaw. "And there are quite a lot of them. They're mostly from Hong Kong, Taiwan or Singapore, but there's an ever increasing number who come from mainland China as well."

Jenkins ran his eyes over the many unintelligible labels on the bottles displayed on the shelves behind the bar. "I haven't a clue what any of those are. So I'll leave it to you, the Chinese booze expert, to make a recommendation."

"Well, since this appears to be your first time in a Chinese bar, perhaps we should stick to Chinese beer," suggested Kershaw. "I think we'd better skip the baijiu."

Jenkins looked puzzled. "What's baijiu?" he asked.

Kershaw smiled. "Something you should never touch on anything less than a full stomach. And there's something else you should......" She was suddenly interrupted by her phone ringing. When she saw the caller's identity she grimaced. "It's the Chief. Sod it. I'm off duty. He can wait."

Jenkins put his hand over Kershaw's phone to stop her rejecting the call. "What was it you were saying earlier about being out of order? Don't you think you should answer it? After all, how much more disappointing do you think it can get?"

There was a further moment's hesitation, before Kershaw finally relented and, through gritted teeth, pressed the call accept button on her phone. She spent the next few minutes doing far more listening than talking, only opening her mouth to utter the occasional, "Yes, Sir"; "Of course, Sir";

or, "Certainly, Sir". As the call continued, the expression on her face slowly changed from one of distaste to a faint smile, although the smile suddenly disappeared just before the call ended.

"Good news?" enquired Jenkins.

"I guess so," Kershaw replied, although sounding far from totally convinced. "It seems I'm back in charge of the case. The Chief said he'd reconsidered his decision after receiving advice, although he didn't say where the advice came from. And he didn't sound too confident about his change of mind either. I got the distinct feeling it was something he'd been pressured into doing. Three times he told me not to let him down. I think once would have been enough, don't you?"

"Absolutely," agreed Jenkins. "But did he have anything to say about me?"

"Yes he did," confirmed Kershaw, with a hint of misgiving still present in her voice. "Right at the end of the call, just before he hung up, he said you would remain involved in the investigation in an advisory role......and that I would be very wise to accept the advice."

Jenkins attempted to reassure her. "It sounds to me like you've got the best of both worlds, DI Kershaw. If the investigation goes well, you can take the credit. But, if it doesn't, you can lay the blame on me. Heads you win, tails I lose."

"That's not quite the way I see it," remarked Kershaw. "And you don't seem to be very surprised by any of this.

That phone-call you made, just before we left the station – that didn't have anything to do with the Chief changing his mind, did it?"

"Almost certainly it did," replied Jenkins. "I rang the person who sent me here to let them know what had happened. They told me they'd quickly get things sorted and I should assume that nothing had changed."

"Whoever they are, they must have a lot of clout," said Kershaw. "Are you going to tell me who it is?"

"I'm afraid I can't," replied Jenkins. "But does that really matter? After all, you're back in charge of the case. You've got what you wanted."

"Okay, so you can't tell me WHO sent you," Kershaw responded, "but can you at least tell me WHY you were sent? Although I haven't mentioned it before, it's been puzzling me ever since you first arrived, why a senior officer from the Met should be sent to help solve a Thames Valley case, especially one that didn't appear to be in any way exceptional. Well, at least not to begin with. And now, after just getting the Chief's phone call, your appearance here seems to be even more mysterious."

Jenkins gave a faint shrug. "To tell you the truth, I'm not entirely clear myself as to why I was sent here, although I intend to find out very soon."

"And then will you tell me?" asked Kershaw.

Jenkins smiled. "I don't know. We'll have to see about that. But in the meantime, acting purely in my advisory role, of course, let me propose an alternative scenario to the one that appears to have already become the received wisdom in this case. At least as far as your Chief Constable is concerned. Consider, for a moment, the possibility that the murder of Charlie Rich has nothing to do with the world of drugs, but everything to do with the contents of Professor Davey's briefcase. Suppose that Charlie was hired to steal it, although he had no idea why. Perhaps he didn't even know the true identity of whoever paid him to carry out the robbery. He only knew he was being well paid for snatching some unsuspecting stranger's bag. Whoever hired Charlie, the inept and drug-addled petty thief, perhaps always expected him to get caught. But what did that matter? If he was dead and unable to talk, the bag snatch would just look like a random street robbery by a well known petty criminal. And Charlie's murder would be assumed to be most probably drugs related and completely unconnected, which, by the way, seems to be what's happened. Obviously, the death of Professor Davey made the bag-snatch a far more serious affair but, from the point of view of whoever hired Charlie, it hasn't changed anything fundamentally."

"You've just described a conspiracy," said Kershaw. "Is that really how you see it?"

"I'm not yet entirely convinced about it. But I certainly think it's a possibility. And one we should consider. You see, I can't understand why Professor Davey would carry around an empty briefcase, especially one that appears to have been locked. I think it's far more likely that it wasn't empty and that whatever it contained was taken away by Charlie Rich's killer. But why would they do that? I know it seems unlikely that a Professor of History would be carrying around anything worth killing for, but that isn't something we should take for granted. On the other hand, of course, I could be totally wrong about everything, and it could all be just one long series of coincidences."

"And where does the envelope stuffed with cash fit into your theory?" asked Kershaw.

"At the moment it doesn't," replied Jenkins with a grin. "I'm still trying to figure it out. I'll let you know when I do."

A widescreen television was positioned high up on the wall at one end of the bar. It was switched on, but the sound was muted. Neither Kershaw nor Jenkins had been paying any attention to it. But when one of the barmen suddenly turned up the volume, they both instinctively turned to look up at the screen. It was the face of Professor Davey that stared back at them.

"It looks like the Chief has finally released his name to the media," said Kershaw.

As Jenkins and Kershaw watched and listened to the news report, they slowly became aware that several of the restaurant staff had come over to join the two barmen. All of them were clearly shocked by what they were seeing on the TV screen.

"Jason, did you know Professor Davey?" Kershaw asked one of the Chinese barmen.

Jason responded with a nod. "Yes. He's been a regular customer of ours ever since we opened, nine years ago. He would often have dinner here with some of his friends and students. We got to know him really well, because whenever he came here he would always chat with me and the other staff, and always in Cantonese. He was really quite fluent in the language."

"And also in Mandarin," added Cheng, the second barman. "Professor Davey was fluent in both languages."

Once the news report of what had happened to Professor Davey had ended, Jason again muted the TV. And the restaurant staff, all quite visibly affected by what they had just seen and heard, slowly returned to their duties.

"Professor Davey is turning out to be a far more interesting character than I'd first imagined," said Jenkins. "And now we're both back on the case I think we should find out a little more about him." He looked at his watch. "It's not very late. We could start right now, by paying a visit to his office at the University?"

"Excellent advice," agreed Kershaw.

It took barely ten minutes to walk the relatively short distance between The Celestial Gardens and Professor Davey's office. On the way over, Kershaw thanked Jenkins for helping to get her put back in charge of the case. "And I suppose I should feel flattered you wanted me reinstated," she said.

"Not necessarily," Jenkins responded casually. "I've met the head of Oxford's Serious Crime Squad. He's got a foul mouth, a disgusting smoker's cough and, even worse, he's a CHIEF Superintendant and outranks me. They're all things that don't apply to you. So I thought you'd be easier to work with."

The sight of Kershaw's Police ID was sufficient to persuade a college porter to hand over the key to Professor Davey's locked office.

"What exactly are we looking for?" Kershaw asked Jenkins as they entered.

"At the moment I have absolutely no idea." Jenkins replied. "But I'm sure I'll recognise it when I see it."

Davey's office had a very definite oriental feel about it. The design of much of the furniture, the style and theme of several of the paintings that hung on the walls, and a number of the ornaments and objects on display, all contributed to that feeling.

Kershaw moved around the room, focussing on nothing in particular, whilst Jenkins concentrated on Davey's desk. Fortunately none of its drawers was locked, and in the very first one he opened he came across the late Professor's desk diary. He was immediately struck by its last entry. It related to the very evening when Davey was killed: *7pm. **Dinner at The Peach Tree with Snoopy.***

Since Davey had been robbed and killed at almost exactly 6.45 pm, Jenkins thought it was reasonable to assume that he must have been on his way to meet his dinner companion at The Peach Tree when it happened. But who the heck was Snoopy?

In the second drawer that Jenkins opened he found half a dozen identical green A4 exercise books. Each of them had the same Chinese character printed on its front cover and none had been written in. He placed them back in the drawer, just as the office door opened and a grim-faced little man entered.

The man was wearing a dinner suit with a purple satin cummerbund and matching bow tie. "May I ask who you are and what you're doing here?" he enquired rather curtly.

Kershaw flashed her Police ID. "Perhaps you could answer the same questions?" she asked.

"I am Sir Peregrine Smythe-Brightly, Professor of Constitutional Law, here at the University," the man responded rather imperiously. "I expect you've heard of me."

Jenkins and Kershaw looked at one another and each shook their head.

"Be that as it may," said Smythe-Brightly dismissively, "I was in my office next door and heard noises in here. Having very recently been made aware of what happened to poor Davey, I knew it couldn't possibly be him. So I came to investigate. I suppose his murder is the reason you two police officers are here."

"Manslaughter," said Kershaw. "We're treating Professor Davey's death as manslaughter. How well did you know him?"

"As well as anyone, I suppose," replied Smythe-Brightly. "We first became acquainted more than thirty years ago, when we were both undergraduates at Balliol. And we've served in the same Faculty and occupied adjacent offices here at the University for the past twenty five years."

"So you should be able to tell us something about his background," said Jenkins. "Do you know if he had any family, for example?"

"None still living, as far as I'm aware," replied Smythe-Brightly. "He was an only child and both his parents are long since dead. And he was a lifelong bachelor, without wife or children. I suppose he could never find the time for that sort of thing, what with all of his obsessions."

"We understand Professor Davey was fluent in both Cantonese and Mandarin. And then there's everything in here," said Kershaw, as she waved her arms around the room. "Was China one of his obsessions?"

"Yes, of course," replied Smythe-Brightly, "and most probably the greatest of them all. The evidence for it is really quite obvious, as you already appear to have discovered. It was something that pervaded every aspect of his life"

Smythe-Brightly held up his hand to show the two police officers the signet ring he was wearing. It was engraved with a single Chinese character. "This was a gift from Davey. He gave it to me at the time I received my knighthood, almost ten years ago, and asked if I'd wear it when I went to the Palace to be shoulder tapped by Her Majesty. It's some sort of Chinese talisman, I believe. Davey was very much into that sort of thing."

"And, somewhere in the drawers of his desk you're sure to come across at least one copy of The Little Red Book. You know, 'The Thoughts of Chairman Mao'. Davey would often pull it out and quote one of its 267 aphorisms. He was particularly keen on those to do with 'correcting mistaken thinking'. I never quite knew whether we were supposed to take him seriously or not. He could be quite inscrutable at times. Although I doubt there were many

Englishmen who understood China and its particular form of communist politics better than he did."

Jenkins was clearly surprised. "Was Professor Davey an admirer of Chinese Communism?" he asked.

"Good Lord, no!" snapped Smythe-Brightly. "I'm fairly certain he despised it. But that didn't stop him finding it a fascinating topic for study. He used to say that it was impossible to truly hate something, unless you properly understood it; until then you could only fear it. But he was very keen on the Chinese people and much of their history and culture. And he was very popular with the University's numerous Chinese students. A few years back they even made him Honorary President of the Chinese Students' Association. Of course, it helped that he could converse with them quite fluently in their own language. You'll find that half the books on the shelves in here are written in one Chinese dialect or another.

"Are you aware of any particular reason why he developed such a special interest in China?" asked Jenkins.

Smythe-Brightly put on a look of great surprise. "My word, you really are in the dark about the man, aren't you. It was because he was born there, of course. Well, to be wholly accurate, he was born in Hong Kong, when it was still a British Crown Colony and part of what remained of the Empire. He once told me that the first words he ever uttered were in Cantonese. It's the main language spoken in Hong Kong and he had a locally recruited nanny who spoke very little English. So I suppose it was inevitable."

Realising that Kershaw and Jenkins knew so very little about Professor Davey, Smythe-Brightly provided them with a brief biography. He explained that at the time of Davey's birth, his father was a senior officer in the Royal Hong Kong Police. During his twenty years in that service he had made many useful contacts within the local business community. When he eventually retired from the RHKP, sometime in the late nineteen seventies, he stayed on in the colony, using those contacts to establish a business of his own. It seems he was one of the first Westerners to correctly anticipate the changes that were about to come in mainland China. And, through a combination of good luck and sound judgement, he succeeded in establishing an import-export business that was to prove extremely profitable.

Davey's arrival at Balliol at the age of eighteen was the beginning of his first extended stay in England. Before then, he'd only ever spent brief periods in the country, usually whilst on vacation with his father. During his first year at Oxford, like most other freshmen, he lived in College, but by the start of his second year he had moved into a house in the city. It was a property bought for him by his wealthy father, one he very quickly filled with imported Chinese furniture and decorations. He even brought his old nanny over from Hong Kong to act as his housekeeper.

Davey's mother appeared to have had very little involvement in her son's life. And from odd comments that Davey had occasionally made, Smythe-Brightly had drawn the clear inference that there had been very little contact between them. Davey had once said that his mother suffered from a multitude of health issues, mostly psychological, and when he was still quite young she had been institutionalised.

No doubt because of the lack of a loving relationship with his biological mother, Davey had grown to be especially close to his nanny, the woman who had played such an important part in his upbringing. Although she never became proficient in English to any great extent, she had remained in Oxford as Davey's housekeeper until her death, which had occurred just ten days earlier. To the end, she had ensured that Davey was always well nourished and his Cantonese remained well practised.

When Davey first arrived at Balliol, Smythe-Brightly said he could detect a slight colonial accent. But he quickly managed to lose it and even began to reinvent himself as a proud Cornishman. His father's family could trace their Cornish roots back through several generations, so he felt his claim was wholly legitimate. He even went to the trouble of learning the Cornish language. Something that even most of those born and bred in the county had failed to do.

The learning of languages was in fact something that came much easier to Davey than to most other people. Perhaps it was because the first language he ever learnt to speak, Cantonese, was so complex. A language with no fewer than nine tones, changes in pitch that affect the meaning of words. But, however he came to possess his remarkable linguistic ability, he put it to good use. At the time of his death, he could speak at least a dozen languages or dialects quite fluently. And he had more than a passing acquaintance with a number of others.

"When did you last speak to Professor Davey?" Jenkins asked.

"It was Monday, the day before yesterday, at exactly four minutes past nine in the morning," replied Smythe-Brightly. "I remember the time so precisely, because I'd only just arrived in my office and barely had time to take off my hat and coat, when he suddenly burst in. He appeared to be in a very agitated state, which was very much out of character. He reckoned that someone had been poking around, both here in his office and in his home, at some time during the weekend."

"Had some things gone missing?" asked Kershaw.

"No, he said that as far as he could tell, nothing had been taken," replied Smythe-Brightly. "But he'd noticed that certain items appeared to have been moved around, like that Chinese vase over there, for example." Smythe-Brightly, pointed to a Blue and White Lotus Pattern Vase that stood on top of a wooden chest. "It's one of a pair. He has an identical one at home. And he'd noticed that both of them had been moved a few inches away from where they should have been."

"Just a few inches!" exclaimed Kershaw in obvious disbelief. "And he reckoned he could still tell they'd been moved?"

"Oh yes," Smythe-Brightly assured her. "Davey was extremely fussy about such matters. He was a great exponent of Feng shui. Everything in here and in his home had to be placed just so."

"Aren't there any CCTV cameras in any of the corridors around here that Professor Davey could have consulted?" asked Jenkins.

"Good heavens no," exclaimed Smythe-Brightly. "The academic staff would never stand for that. This is a university, not a high security prison. There are closed circuit TV cameras in most of the administrative areas, and around and about outside, but nowhere else."

Smythe-Brightly looked at his watch. "Oh dear, this has taken up far more time than I had realised. If there's nothing else, constables, I really should take my leave. I have a dinner engagement in less than ten minutes, with a very senior member of the judiciary."

Jenkins still had one last question to ask. "Just before you go, Sir Peregrine. Do you know anyone who Professor Davey might refer to as Snoopy?"

Kershaw had not seen the entry in the desk diary so, quite understandably, she was somewhat bemused by Jenkins' question. And she was almost equally surprised by the answer he received.

"Yes, as a matter of fact I do," replied Smythe-Brightly. "He was a fellow student when Davey and I were undergraduates at Balliol. His name is Algernon St John Fairfax. I believe Davey did keep in touch with him after we all graduated. Last I heard of him he'd joined the Royal Navy. But what he does these days I have no idea. Unlike Davey, I never bothered to keep connected. I always thought Fairfax to be a rather tiresome, pompous little man. Why do you ask?"

"Just routine questioning," said Jenkins, with the hint of a smirk. "Thank you Sir Peregrine, you've been extremely helpful. We were very lucky that you were still in your office when we arrived."

"You are in fact quite exceptionally lucky," said Smythe-Brightly. "I first left the premises a couple of hours ago. But then I had to pop back to collect my mobile phone, which I had rather carelessly left on my office desk."

Smythe-Brightly left the room and Kershaw closed the door behind him. "What an egotistical and self important little man," she said. "Why on earth would he assume we'd heard of him?"

"Actually, I have heard of him," said Jenkins. "But I wasn't going to stroke his ego by letting him know that. I've seen him on TV a couple of times. He's one of those so-called experts they wheel out, every now and again, to talk knowledgeably about something or other. In his case it's the British Constitution."

"And where the heck did Snoopy come from?" asked Kershaw.

Jenkins showed her the entry in Davey's desk diary. "Something for me to follow up," he said. "Perhaps you could take the Blue and White Lotus Pattern Vase and get it checked for fingerprints. And do the same with the one he kept in his home. If Davey was right, and someone really was rummaging around in here and at his home, it's more than likely they'd be wearing gloves, but, you never know, there's always a chance they got careless."

Continuing his search through Davey's desk drawers, Jenkins soon came across a copy of The Little Red Book that

Smythe-Brightly had mentioned. It had clearly been well used and there were numerous handwritten Chinese characters drawn in the margin of each of its pages. Jenkins thought that perhaps they expressed Professor Davey's own view of the particular aphorism alongside which they were drawn, although he could not, of course, be certain of this.

What Jenkins was sure of, though, was that the Chinese character Professor Davey had written most frequently in the margin of his copy of Mao's Little Red Book, was the same one he'd just seen engraved on Smythe-Brightly's signet ring. Rather intrigued by this fact, he thought he'd see if he could find out what the character signified, so very carefully made a copy of it in his police notebook.

After finding nothing else of interest in any of the desk drawers, Jenkins returned to thumbing his way through the pages of Professor Davey's desk diary. And he soon came across a second entry that caught his attention. It was dated just a few days before Davey was killed: *Prinsted – to see Dr James Caulfield.* This particular entry he did not show to DI Kershaw.

It was now getting late. Having decided that both he and Kershaw could probably do with a good night's sleep, Jenkins suggested they call it a day.

"That thing I didn't know I was looking for," he said, as he pocketed Professor Davey's desk diary, "I believe I've just found it…. and one or two other things besides."

Brazelle was out on a dinner date with his fiancée, Rose Harfield, when Jenkins phoned to tell him about Davey's planned meeting with James Caulfield, someone Brazelle knew well. It was an entirely unexpected development, which Brazelle knew nothing about. He promised to follow it up the next morning.

"That was Chief Inspector Jenkins, wasn't it?" said Rose, as Brazelle returned his phone to his pocket. "I heard you call him Ifor."

"Yes it was, although it's **Superintendent** Jenkins these days."

"Well, that's certainly quick promotion," remarked Rose. "He was still only an Inspector when I first met him. And that was just a few months back. I assume his rapid rise through the ranks is all due to his involvement in the Gant case. Is that why he called you? Has there been some progress in identifying Gant's assassin?"

"No," Brazelle replied. "He phoned about an entirely different matter. And, as it happens, due to a lack of any useful leads, they started scaling back the hunt for Gant's killer about a week ago. Ifor Jenkins has only been marginally involved with the case since then. In fact, at the moment, he's temporarily based in Oxford, helping Thames Valley Police with a couple of their cases."

"Do you think that means they'll soon give up trying to find out who killed Gant altogether?" asked Rose.

Brazelle gave a faint shrug. "Who knows? But I doubt they'll give up just yet. It was always going to be a tough case to solve. And I reckon it's been made even more difficult because the investigating team's been working on a false premise. They seem fixated on the notion that Gant's killer was contracted by the criminal organisation he'd been working for. But the reason they had for wanting him dead was to stop him talking. And that motive had well and truly disappeared by the time he was killed. By then, the organisation was almost completely dismantled and its leaders were all dead. And just about all of its other members had been identified and were either already in custody or being hunted down. What purpose would Gant's death serve then? There was nothing he could possibly have said that would have made a blind bit of difference to anything."

"So, if it wasn't to stop him talking, what do you think was the motive for Gant's assassination?" asked Rose.

"Revenge," replied Brazelle. "I have no doubt about it. God alone knows how many secrets Gant must have revealed and individuals he betrayed. Once his treachery became known, there would have been any number of people with a motive for killing him. People like me, for example. It was almost certainly Gant who betrayed my team in South Africa, seven years ago. I lost five good friends that day, another one lost an eye and I almost lost my own life."

"And I guess you could put me on the list as well," said Rose. "I've also got a strong motive for wanting revenge against Gant. He was the man who betrayed my father and gave the order for him to be killed." Rose paused for a moment. "Do you think you could still love me if I was the assassin?" she asked.

"Why? Were you?"

Rose was taken by surprise. "I was hoping for a simple, 'Yes, of course, darling'. What caused that unexpected reaction?"

"I wanted to know if we were talking hypothetically or for real."

"Does that mean you think I'm capable of killing someone?"

"Not necessarily," Brazelle replied. "But an army's ranks aren't filled with psychopaths. Some of the things I witnessed in the military convinced me that, given the right circumstances, just about anyone would be capable of violence, even extreme violence. Although it's far from being the only one, the desire for revenge can be a very strong motivator. There may well be some total pacifists in the world, but I'm convinced that I've never met one. As for you personally, remember I was there in Cromwell's Treasure that Sunday lunchtime, soon after we first met, when you beat up those three male delinquents. And it didn't look to me like it was something you were doing for the first time in your life. It's true that what I witnessed you do that day came as a big surprise, but it would take a lot more than that to change the way I feel about you."

"Okay, so forgetting about me for the moment, have you any other thoughts on who the assassin might be?" asked Rose.

"Only that they'd have to be an expert sniper, very likely someone with military training," Brazelle replied.

"I guess so," agreed Rose. "An eight hundred metre shot with an M24. That's just about its limit of accuracy."

"That's right," confirmed Brazelle, clearly surprised by Rose's knowledge of the ballistic capabilities of an M24 sniper rifle. But that wasn't the only thing that surprised him.

"I've just had an idea," said Rose. "Why don't we invite Ifor Jenkins to join us for dinner at Harfield House, one evening next week? Say Tuesday? We haven't seen him in a while. Perhaps he'll give us an update on the search for Gant's assassin."

DAY THREE – THURSDAY

Dr James Caulfield, a widower in his late seventies, lives alone in a thatched stone cottage on the western edge of Prinsted. For more than forty years he had served as the Prinsted village doctor, a position filled by generations of his ancestors before him. And when he retired, a little over five years ago, he was succeeded in the role by his son, Gerald.

Caulfield's cottage was originally built by his eight times great grandfather, Alexander De Calvairac, a Huguenot refugee from France, soon after he and his family arrived in Prinsted, in the late 1620's. For almost three centuries, the cottage remained the home of the De Calvairac – Caulfield family, until, at the beginning of the twentieth century, James Caulfield's great grandfather, Dr Edward Caulfield, closed up its shutters for the last time, and moved his young and growing family to a much larger and far grander home in the centre of the village. Over the decades that followed, the property was left mainly at the mercy of nature and the elements, with only minimal maintenance undertaken to prevent its total demise. Until, that is, a little over five years ago when James Caulfield began restoring his modest ancestral residence to its former glory, augmented through the addition of all the usual modern amenities. Once the job was completed, he made the cottage his home.

Prior to Jenkins' phone call the previous evening, Brazelle had no knowledge of any contact having taken place between Professor Davey and Dr James Caulfield. And he was surprised to learn there had been. It seemed to be such an unlikely coincidence, that Davey should meet with a member of one of Prinsted's most prominent families, whilst carrying out research on another, unless, of course, there was a connection. But what might that be? Brazelle was certainly keen to find out, though wanting to do it without making James Caulfield aware of his curiosity. To do otherwise, he thought, would likely elicit a flurry of questions that he had no wish to answer. But he would not stoop to telling lies, least of all to someone he regarded as a friend. It was clear he needed a plan that would allow him to tell the truth and nothing but the truth, although, perhaps, not the whole truth.

A keen and skilled artist, Brazelle has a particular interest in architectural structures and buildings, especially those that come with an exceptional history and are in some way unique. James Caulfield's seventeenth century cottage certainly ticked all the right boxes. Brazelle had visited the property a number of times over recent years and seen it at various stages of its restoration. And on more than one of those occasions he'd expressed an interest in painting it and adding its image to his collection, once all the work was completed. So far, the many other demands made on his time had prevented him from even beginning the task but, given current circumstances, he considered it was now a matter to which he could very conveniently turn his attention.

Being aware that James Caulfield was an early riser, Brazelle phoned him, just as soon as he himself woke, and arranged to visit him at his cottage later that morning. When he arrived, carrying a camera, a sketch pad and some pencils, he found Caulfield in his garden, feeding some chickens.

"I'm aiming at self-sufficiency," Caulfield explained. "I've got my bees and now I've invested in a few chickens. I may very well have a couple of goats and the beginnings of an orchard by this time next year. Assuming I'm still here, that is!"

Caulfield stopped what he was doing and led the way into the cottage's very modern looking lounge.

Brazelle's previous visits to Caulfield's cottage had all been very brief affairs, and the lounge was the only room he had ever been inside. Today, though, in addition to hopefully finding out why Professor Davey had paid Caulfield a visit, he anticipated seeing the rest of the cottage's interior, as well as learning rather more about the property's history. In effect, he would be killing two birds with one stone.

"What exactly do you already know about the history of my family and this cottage?" Caulfield asked.

"Only what Gerald's told me," Brazelle replied. "That the house was originally built by your ancestor, Alexander De Calvairac, a French Huguenot refugee, sometime in the late sixteen twenties and that it remained the De Calvairac family home until your great grandfather more or less abandoned it, around 1900. Gerald also told me that the family name was changed from De Calvairac to the more English sounding Caulfield during the Napoleonic Wars, because of the anti-French feeling that developed in the country around that time."

"Well, if that's the full extent of what Gerald told you I can see there are a number of gaps to be filled and at least one correction to be made," said Caulfield. "For a start, the house was never abandoned. My great grandfather always intended to return to live here. He chose to temporarily close it up and move to a larger property in the village, because of his growing family. At the time he moved out he already had a son, my grandfather, and a daughter. And his wife was pregnant with twin girls. My grandfather claimed that it was always his father's intention to one day return and take up residence again, but only after his children were grown up and all safely married off. Because that was his plan, he didn't bother taking all of his furniture with him when he moved out and he frequently visited the place to make sure it was well maintained. Unfortunately, he died when he was still a relatively young man and never got the opportunity to return to live here. It was only after his death that the rot began to set in, so to speak. My grandfather was only an infant when the family moved out so had no memory of ever living here. And my father never lived in the property. I assume that's why neither of them ever appeared to have much of an attachment to the place. It probably also explains why they didn't take as much care of it as my great grandfather had done. In fact I often wonder why they didn't just sell the place. But I'm very glad they didn't."

"Perhaps they had a subconscious emotional attachment to it," suggested Brazelle. "Given its place in your family's history, it would be surprising if it didn't have some kind of hold on them."

"Maybe," said Caulfield, "but I don't recall either my grandfather or my father ever talking much about it. I was almost ten years old when my grandfather first brought me here, although for what reason I don't recall. That was the first time I got to see the house, or even learn of its existence. Coming inside was like stepping back in time. I can still remember the thick dark curtains that were drawn over the windows and the faded wallpaper, although I could still just about make out its pattern of large flowers. And, of course, there was the furniture that looked like it should have been in a museum. The place totally fascinated me and I secretly committed to one day restoring the place and living here."

"What did you do with the furniture your great grandfather left here, when you did your restoration?" Brazelle asked.

"That's a very good question," replied Caulfield with a broad smile. "Come with me."

Caulfield led the way out of the lounge and down a short corridor to a room at the end. Brazelle was amazed by what he saw inside. The room was panelled throughout in dark oak and contained a magnificent four poster bed. A few other matching pieces of furniture were also present. There were two chairs, a dresser and a desk, although the four-poster was the room's most dominant feature.

The room was illuminated by light through its single window, which was fitted with wooden shutters and a pair of thick dark curtains. As Brazelle took his time looking around, two things soon struck him. Firstly, there was no sign of electric switches, sockets or lights. And secondly, the room's dark oak panelling appeared to be identical to that which he had seen in the old basement at Harfield House. Was that mere coincidence?

"As you might imagine, Chris, the house has been altered a good deal over the centuries. But as far I've been able to tell, this room appears to have been tinkered with the least. I've attempted to restore it to what it might well have looked like when Alexander De Calvairac lived here, almost four hundred years ago. The furniture, I am assured by the experts who cleaned and restored it, dates from that period. It's what was left in the house when my great grandfather moved out. It intrigues me to think that it was almost certainly used by Alexander and his family. In fact he probably slept in this very bed. But this is not all I have to show you. There's one other feature you might find interesting."

Caulfield moved to stand at the head of the bed. "As you well know Chris, religious persecution is as old as religion itself and Alexander De Calvairac had first-hand experience of it. In 1623, he was one of the leaders of an uprising, near La Rochelle in south-west France, against the religious tyranny of the Catholic French King. However, the insurrection failed, and Alexander became a hunted man who, together with his wife and children, was forced to flee for his life. According to family tradition, his death warrant was signed by Cardinal Richelieu himself. But whether that particular detail is true or not, there can be little doubt that what Alexander and his family endured as fugitives, fleeing their homeland, would have had a lasting effect on them. And they probably continued to harbour the fear that it could all happen again. I believe that Alexander very likely still had such concerns on his mind when he built this house. And that's why he created..........this."

Caulfield reached into the space behind the bed and pulled a small, barely visible, lever. One of the oak panels in the adjacent wall immediately came away, to reveal a small compartment that was previously hidden behind.

It appeared to Brazelle that the compartment was in exactly the same position as the one he'd discovered behind the panelling in the old basement of Harfield House and looked to be identical to it in size. Was this just another coincidence? Or was the creation of the one in the basement of Harfield House inspired by the one here that almost certainly predated it.

"Have you always known the compartment was there?" Brazelle asked.

"No, not at all," replied Caulfield. "It's a very recent discovery. I more or less stumbled across it during the final stages of the cottage's restoration work. I believe it was where Alexander kept what we would call today his grab-box. The box that contained his most treasured possessions and the one thing he would be sure to seize and take with him if he ever again needed to flee for his life."

When first discovered, the equivalent compartment in the basement of Harfield House was found to contain two items, both of which had meant a great deal to Sir Richard Harfield. There was a golden phalera that had been given to him when he was just nine years old, by the dying Royalist soldier, Captain John Hadlington. And there was a leather belt that carried two holstered pistols and a dagger in its sheath, bequeathed to him by his adoptive father, Reverend Richard Shuttleworth. Their presence in the hidden compartment had puzzled Brazelle, but now he believed he understood why they were there. If the time ever came when Sir Richard and his family needed to flee, through the tunnel that led out of the basement of Harfield House, then they were the last things he would grab and take with him as he made his escape.

Caulfield picked up a wooden box with a hinged lid that was standing on the desk and opened it. "I found this inside the hidden compartment. It has Alexander's initials carved on the lid, so I think there's a good chance it's his grab-box. I didn't find any treasure in it, but it wasn't completely empty, as it is now. It contained three scrolled parchments, each tied with a pink ribbon. Unfortunately, the writing on them was extremely faded, so none of them was entirely readable. But odd words that were visible made it clear they were all written in French."

Brazelle's ears picked up at the mention of parchments, but something puzzled him. "I can understand your great grandfather leaving some furniture behind when he moved home, especially if he intended to return at some point, but I'm very surprised he left family documents, particularly if they were considered important enough to store in a grab-box in a hidden compartment?"

"I agree," said Caulfield, "but he may not have known they were there, or even known about the compartment. As I said, I only found it quite by chance. The small lever you saw me pull to expose it was fitted there by me. The one that was there originally must have been either accidentally broken off, or deliberately removed. But who knows when or by whom? It's possible that knowledge of the compartment and its contents was lost many years ago, well before even my great grandfather's time. A family secret can soon be lost if one generation fails to pass it on to the next. Of course there are many reasons why that might happen. When I first discovered the parchments they were a complete mystery to me. But I've learnt something about them since then."

Caulfield smiled as he moved to the door. "I can tell you're interested, Chris. So follow me."

Caulfield led the way out of the restored ground floor bedroom and into the adjacent very modern looking dining room. Three identical picture frames hung side by side on one of the walls. The frame in the middle was empty, whilst each of the other two contained the remains of a parchment. The text on each of the parchments was faded, in some places almost to the point of invisibility. And there was the occasional lacuna where the parchment had completely disintegrated and simply disappeared. Brazelle took a moment to study each of them in turn. But he failed to make any sense of either, except to confirm what he had already been told, that they were both written in French.

"Given their poor condition you're probably wondering why I had them framed and hung on the wall," said Caulfield.

"You read my mind," responded Brazelle, before pointing to the empty frame. "And whilst we're on the subject, what happened to the third one?"

"I put them up there as conversation pieces," Caulfield replied with a grin. "I was hoping their appearance would prove exceptional enough to get them noticed and commented upon by one or two of my occasional dinner guests. And I thought that might possibly lead to a more interesting discussion over dinner than might otherwise be the case. Some of my friends can be rather dull conversationalists, you know."

Caulfield let out a giggle, before adopting a more serious tone. "But, as for the missing third parchment, well, to be honest, Chris, I'm beginning to wonder if I'll ever see it again. It was taken away to be restored and hopefully translated and made sense of by the same person who provided me with information on the other two remaining parchments. I doubt you know him, but I'm sure you'll recognise his name. It's been all over the news ever since yesterday evening. He's the poor chap who was killed in a street robbery in Oxford two days ago, Professor Graham Davey."

Brazelle had been struggling to think of some plausibly innocent way of bringing Davey's name into the conversation, which was of course his real reason for being there. All of a sudden his problem was unexpectedly solved and he moved quickly to exploit his opportunity. "Actually, I had heard of Professor Davey before hearing the news of his unfortunate death. He was a Professor of History at Oxford, wasn't he? Did you consult him to get his help with the parchments?"

"No, that was mere coincidence," replied Caulfield. "It was Davey who first got in touch with me. I'd never even heard of the chap before then. He said he was creating a compendium of unusual stories dating from the English Civil War. And he wanted to include the tale of how Prinsted's village tavern came to be given the name Cromwell's Treasure. With my family's many years of residence in Prinsted, stretching back to a few decades before that time, he reckoned I was probably the ideal person to consult on the matter. My initial reaction was to suggest he look elsewhere. I told him there were many others in the village who were at least as knowledgeable on the subject as I was. I even suggested he might consider approaching the Harfield family, seeing as how they actually own the tavern. But he was very insistent. He intrigued me by mentioning one or two things about my ancestors that even I didn't know. It sounded very much to me like he'd made a study of the De Calvairac-Caulfield family history before he got in touch with me. So, eventually, I gave in and agreed to see him. He came over last Saturday. I doubt I told him very much about Cromwell's Treasure that he didn't already know, but he was certainly very helpful with the parchments. It came as a terrible shock when I heard on the news that the poor chap had been killed."

Caulfield pointed to one of the parchments on the wall. "According to Professor Davey, that one's a land sale receipt and dates to sometime in the early seventeenth century. I suppose today we'd call it some sort of conveyance document. The other one dates to the same period. Davey said it's a document confirming ownership of a building and some land. I guess, today, we'd call it the property's Deeds. He thought it likely that the two documents relate to the same property, although to be sure of that, or to determine anything else about either of them, he said he would have to take them away and give them both a bit of TLC. But, quite frankly, he didn't appear too interested in doing that. It was only when he came to take a closer look at the third parchment, the one he ended up taking away with him, that he began to show a degree of real excitement. He said it was written much later than the other two, in the year 1685, but he couldn't be more specific about either the document's date, or its purpose, without having some restorative work done on it. And this time he appeared extremely keen to do that. He said it would take a few days to get the job done properly and then he'd be back in touch. After I got over the shock of hearing about his death, I was initially at a bit of a loss as to what to do about the parchment. But then I decided to leave it for a few days before contacting the university to see if they can track it down. Given the circumstances, I thought it would be rather unseemly and in bad taste to chase it up any sooner. Having said that though, I am rather concerned it might end up going astray or, worse still, perhaps end up being destroyed."

"How did you get onto the subject of the parchments with Professor Davey?" asked Brazelle. "Was it quite by chance?"

Caulfield shook his head. "No, I wouldn't exactly say it was by chance. Davey commented on my ancestors having lived in the same village, and even in this same property, over many generations. He said it made him wonder if, in addition to some furniture and the house itself, any documents had also survived through the ages. If they had, he said, he would be extremely interested in taking a look at them. I remember him saying that, 'Documents can be as manna from Heaven for any historian'. At the time, it didn't strike me as anything other than an innocent enough question for the man to ask. After all, he was a historian. And that's when I showed him the parchments. It was only later, when I thought back to the way our conversation had developed, led mainly by him, that I began to think the parchments, or at least the one he took away with him to be restored, were the real reason he came to see me. But then I wondered how he got to know I had it, or even suspect that I did. After all, I only found the parchments, myself, a few weeks ago. Since then the only person I've shown them to, or even mentioned them to, is Gerald. And he didn't seem too interested. It was all very odd. When I was a GP I quite frequently had a patient consult me, seemingly about some minor ailment, only to discover that the real reason was something entirely different. Very often it would be a middle aged man, who supposedly came to consult me on something or other, before moving the conversation very quickly to the matter of his erectile dysfunction, the real reason he wanted to see me. It happened so often I got to develop an instinct for such subterfuge."

Brazelle considered the possibility that Caulfield was indirectly telling him he'd been rumbled and that he knew his proposed artwork was not the real reason for his visit. In an effort to convince him otherwise, Brazelle spent a couple of hours taking photographs and making sketches of various parts of the cottage, both inside and out. Before leaving, he explained that the photographs and sketches would form the basis of a painting, or possibly two, that he would complete over the coming weeks.

As he drove home, Brazelle wondered if the document Professor Davey mentioned in his phone call was the parchment he had taken from James Caulfield to be restored. It certainly seemed likely. But what was it? And, if Caulfield was right about the parchment being Davey's real reason for paying him a visit, how did Davey come to know about it? Or, was it all mere coincidence? With Davey dead and unable to be quizzed on the matter, the only route to finding answers appeared to lie with the parchment itself.

Soon after arriving home, Brazelle phoned Jenkins to report on his visit to James Caulfield and told him about the missing parchment. Jenkins promised to see if he could track it down during his next visit to the University, which he planned on making later that day.

On his first day at boarding school, Algernon St John Fairfax, aged just seven and rather gangly, was informed by the older boys that the adoption of a nickname was obligatory. He chose Snoopy, considering it to be the least offensive of the limited number of options he was given.

After that, since every new chapter of his life overlapped to some extent with the previous one, he was never able to make an entirely clean break with the past, and consequently, the nickname stuck. It even followed him into the Royal Navy, which he joined immediately after graduating from Oxford with an upper second in Mathematics.

Proving himself to be an able and competent naval officer, Fairfax rose to the rank of Commander and was about to be given his first command, as Captain of a frigate, when his seafaring days were brought to an abrupt and unexpected end. He was involved in an unfortunate incident that left him unable to walk without the aid of a stick. It was an affliction he would forever after refer to as his 'war wound'. The truth, however, sounded significantly less heroic. He had fallen off his bike whilst cycling to the butchers on an errand for his wife.

Still a relatively young man when he was declared unfit for sea-going duties, Fairfax was transferred to a desk job in Naval Intelligence, a development he had neither anticipated nor desired, but one that proved to be most fortuitous. It turned out that he had a particular gift for intelligence work and, consequently, he excelled in his new role.

Fifteen years on, and Fairfax had progressed to become head of his own department, Naval Intelligence Asia Pacific, with the title of Assistant Director. He was also the person responsible for Superintendent Ifor Jenkins becoming involved with the Davey case.

As soon as Jenkins was shown into Fairfax's office he wasted no time in getting to the point. "Why didn't you tell me Professor Davey was a friend of yours?" he asked curtly. "And that he was on his way to meet you when he was killed?"

"For the very simple reason that you didn't need to know," Fairfax replied equally abruptly. "All you were being asked to do was determine whether or not the attack on Davey was a purely chance event and, if at all possible, retrieve the contents of his briefcase. Beyond that, there was nothing further you needed to be told, at least not at that point. Anyway, where did your information about me come from?"

"Your planned meeting was noted in Davey's desk diary, where he'd identified you as Snoopy," Jenkins replied. "Everything else, I got to know from Sir Peregrine Smythe-Brightly."

Fairfax gave a faint sneer at the mention of Smythe-Brightly's name. "So, you got to meet that puffed-up waste of a well tailored suit. I hope you enjoyed the experience."

Jenkins ignored Fairfax's obvious contempt for Smythe-Brightly and steered the conversation back to the reason for his visit. "Perhaps you can at least tell me why I was given this job in the first place. If it's so highly confidential why didn't you give it to one of your own people?"

"Good Lord, I couldn't possibly have done that," replied Fairfax, aghast. "I'm trying my best to keep this whole affair as low-key as possible. If the media got to hear that someone from Naval Intelligence or, for that matter, any other intelligence service, was taking an interest in a street robbery in Oxford, and believe me they would, and pretty damn quick too, what on earth do you think they'd make of it? Not to mention the internet blogging conspiracy theorists. No, to minimise the chances of drawing any unwanted attention to the case it had to be a bona fide police officer who was given the commission. And it had to be one who'd already been proved capable of dealing efficiently and confidentially with a particularly sensitive matter. That's why you were chosen. You're a senior police officer who was very recently well and truly road tested in the Gant case. Lord knows, it's risky enough having you involved but, given the urgency of getting a grip on the situation, you were the best available."

"Thanks for the vote of confidence," Jenkins remarked wryly. "But what did you need to tell the Met Commissioner and the Chief Constable of Thames Valley to get them both to agree to have me on the case?"

"Nothing," Fairfax replied bluntly. "Neither of them has an inkling of what this is all about. I went over their heads. It's amazing what can be speedily achieved with the use of those six little words: **in the interests of national security**. At the moment less than a dozen people know the full facts. In this country that is! By now I imagine significantly more people are aware in China."

The reference to China left Jenkins totally bemused. "China! What the hell has China got to do with it?"

Fairfax leaned forward over his desk. "What do you know about the Chinese structure of government?" he asked.

"A lot less than you, I suspect," replied Jenkins.

Fairfax took a photograph out of his desk drawer and handed it to Jenkins. It was a line-up of seven dark suited Chinese men, all clearly of pensionable or near pensionable age. And not one could have looked more stoney-faced and joyless, even if attending their best friend's funeral.

"These are the seven members of the Standing Committee of the Chinese Communist Party's Politburo," Fairfax explained. "They're the men who rule China. And, take it from me, nothing of any importance happens in that country without their say-so. They're not a particularly publicity-seeking bunch, at least not outside China, so it's likely that the only one of them you might possibly recognise is the chap in the middle. He's the boss, the top-man who wields the absolute power to hire and fire any of the other six at will. An individual's proximity to him in the photograph is significant. The closer he is to the boss, the more important and influential he is. Take a look at the man standing immediately to the top-man's right. His name is Li Yibo."

"They all look like as if their dog's just died," commented Jenkins. "What's so special about Li Yibo?"

"Well, for a start, he's the only one of them who's now dead," said Fairfax. "But I'll get to that matter in a minute. First, though, I need to be sure you understand that not a word of what I'm about to tell you should ever be repeated outside this room."

Jenkins gave the required assurance and Fairfax began his narrative with a reference to something that had happened four days earlier, on the previous Sunday, in one of the Chinese government offices in Zhongnanhai, Beijing. It was an event at which each of the seven men in the photograph was given a copy of a rather thick document to read, prior to the group giving it their collective approval.

Li Yibo took his copy home, told his family and servants that he didn't want to be disturbed and went into his study to read it through. A few hours later, when he failed to turn up for dinner, his twenty five year old son went to find out why and found his father dead.

The son was aware that his father had been receiving treatment for a fairly serious heart condition for several years. And, since there was absolutely no hint of foul play, he assumed that the old man had finally succumbed to his affliction.

Understandably upset by this shocking discovery, the son's distress was made even worse when he realised the nature of the document that his father had been reading when he died. In fact, it had such a disturbing effect on him that he didn't immediately report his father's death. Instead, he informed the servants and other family members that his father would not be coming to dinner and wished to remain in his study, undisturbed.

The son then made a show of taking a tray of food and drink into his father's study, before hurriedly, yet discreetly, leaving the house and heading for the nearest airport, taking with him the document that his father had been reading.

There are numerous advantages to being the son of a member of the Chinese ruling elite. Not least of which is the possession of a passport that permits total freedom of travel, both domestically and internationally. At the airport, Li Yibo's son was therefore able to buy a ticket on the next available flight out of China. He deliberately chose a non-Chinese airline, opting for a scheduled Lufthansa flight, travelling direct to Frankfurt.

The son assumed it wouldn't be until the next morning that his father's body would be discovered. After that, he thought it probable that a few more hours would likely pass, before the authorities eventually realised what he had done. By then he expected to be well outside Chinese airspace. As it turned out, by the time the Chinese authorities fully grasped what had happened, and raised the alarm, he had already landed at Frankfurt and boarded a connecting flight to Heathrow.

Within barely twenty four hours of discovering his father was dead, Li Yibo's son arrived in Oxford, where he went directly to the home of Professor Graham Davey. The document he'd brought with him was written in Mandarin, a language in which the Professor was fluent. Davey only needed to read the first few pages before realising the document's significance. At which point, with his young friend's agreement, he phoned Commander Fairfax.

Jenkins listened attentively to Fairfax's narrative and was struck by the amount of detail he'd included. "How did you get to know all of this?" he asked.

"Mostly from what Li Yibo's son told Davey," Fairfax replied, "although he wasn't the only source. After Li Yibo was found dead and the Chinese authorities realised his son, and the document, had both gone missing, it quickly dawned on them what must have happened. That's when all hell broke loose, leading to a dramatic increase in signals traffic. GCHQ constantly monitor what's happening in China and they picked up some of it. What they managed to gather didn't tell them anything about the nature of the missing document, but it did confirm that Li Yibo was dead and that the son had gone AWOL, with something the Chinese were desperate to get back."

"Are you going to tell me anything else about this document?" asked Jenkins. "Like what it is, for example?"

"I'm afraid not, old boy," replied Fairfax with a grin. "But, in any case, I can't see there's anything more I can say that would be helpful to you. After all, the document is written in Mandarin, a language you can't read or understand."

Jenkins was naturally curious to know why Li Yibo's son had chosen to fly half way round the world with the document and then give it to Professor Davey.

Fairfax explained that the son had been a student at Oxford for the past six years. Initially it was as an undergraduate, but currently he was studying for a doctorate in International Law. During his time at the University he'd got to know Davey well and they had become friends, with Davey taking on the role of something akin to an unofficial mentor.

"Given the situation the young man found himself in, no doubt Davey was the most obvious person for him to confide in," said Fairfax. "Davey was a westerner whom

Li Yibo's son had grown to trust and admire. And he either knew, or assumed, correctly as it happens, that he had some useful contacts."

"And you're one of those useful contacts," remarked Jenkins.

"So it would seem," agreed Fairfax. "Davey and I have been friends since our student days and he knew I worked in Naval Intelligence. That's why he brought the matter to me. I suggested putting him in touch with someone from MI6, but he said he would only pass the document directly to me. When he first contacted me I was in America, so I flew back as quickly as possible, taking the next available flight. I arranged to see him later the same evening, at the place where we usually met, The Peach Tree. It's just a twenty five minute stroll from Davey's office at the University. At that stage, the only person I informed was the Head of Naval Intelligence. He then took it up the food chain through to the Secretary of State for Defence and, eventually, the Prime Minister. It was then agreed we should keep it amongst ourselves, at least until we made sure it wasn't some elaborately contrived hoax. In the intervening period Li Yibo's son disappeared from Oxford leaving the document with Davey, which understandably made the poor chap even more anxious. Then, when his briefcase was stolen, whilst he was on his way to meet me, we didn't know whether it was an unfortunate coincidence or a targeted attack. Something we were keen to find out. As I'm sure you can understand, we were also pretty anxious to retrieve the contents of Davey's briefcase. And that's where you come in. We reckoned you gave us our best chance of achieving both those objectives, with only the minimum of fuss. It was the PM who suggested using you, by the way.

He said he'd been very impressed by how you'd handled the Gant case. But don't let that go to your head. It's the only affair of its kind that's happened on the current PM's watch. Thank God! So he hasn't exactly got much of a standard to judge you by."

The rather smug look that had begun to appear on Jenkins' face at the mention of the Prime Minister's endorsement suddenly vanished. "When did you first find out about the attack on Davey?" he asked.

"Fortunately, it wasn't very long after it happened," replied Fairfax. "Davey was always very punctual, so I started to get a bit concerned when it got to five past seven and he still hadn't arrived at The Peach Tree, especially given the reason for our planned meeting. So I called his phone and, to my surprise, it was a paramedic who answered. That's when I found out that Davey was dead, after what was assumed to be a street robbery, and that his briefcase was missing."

"Do you suspect the Chinese?" asked Jenkins.

Fairfax shook his head. "No, I don't. And, quite frankly, nobody else involved with this case does either. For a start, there wasn't enough time between them realising the document had gone missing with Li Yibo's son and the attack on Davey taking place. In that time they would have had to track the son, finger Davey as the holder of the document and then set up the attack. The Chinese Intelligence services are good, but they're not that good. Anyway, even if that was all possible, the Chinese would never have tried to recover the document through a street bag-snatch, let alone hire someone like Charlie Rich to carry out the job. Believe me Superintendent Jenkins, if the Chinese got to know or even just suspect, that Davey had the document, they would have dealt with him immediately and directly. We're well aware they already have a good number of their people in this country who are more than capable of getting their property back, and certainly without the need for any bag-snatch shenanigans. But there's also another reason for thinking it wasn't the Chinese. Since the attack on Davey and the murder of Charlie Rich, the volume of Chinese signals traffic hasn't reduced. In fact it's increased. All the signs are that they're still looking for the missing document."

"So, if it wasn't the Chinese, is there anyone else you suspect?" asked Jenkins.

"At the moment, we have nobody specific in mind," replied Fairfax. "But given what happened to Charlie Rich and the fact that the document has gone missing, we have to consider the possibility that some other player is involved. What do Thames Valley Police think?"

"They seem convinced that Davey was a randomly chosen victim and that Charlie Rich's murder was drugs related and totally unconnected," Jenkins replied.

"From their point of view that must seem like the most reasonable working premise," suggested Fairfax. "After all, they don't know anything about a missing Chinese document. But it really doesn't matter what Thames Valley Police think. You're the one who is effectively in charge of the case and can steer the investigation in any direction you want. I made sure of that. Of course it's still possible that Thames Valley has got it right. Maybe the two events are completely unrelated."

"If that is the case, then where's the Chinese document?" asked Jenkins. "What are the chances that a professional killer would remove an unknown and unreadable document from the scene of their crime?"

"Perhaps it wasn't unreadable," suggested Fairfax. "Maybe the killer could read Mandarin and realised its potential value?"

"Now that really would be a coincidence," said Jenkins.

After leaving Fairfax, Jenkins returned to Oxford and went directly to Professor Davey's office at the University, intending to explore the place a little further. He had also promised Brazelle that he would try to track down James Caulfield's parchment and thought Professor Davey's office was a good place to start.

He began his exploration by taking a closer look at the chest upon which the Blue and White Lotus Pattern Vase had stood. Lifting the lid, he found it contained more than thirty green A4 exercise books. They were identical to those he had seen in Davey's desk drawer on his previous visit, although these were not unused. They were all filled with copious handwritten notes, mostly written in English but some in Chinese. And there was a date written on the spine of each of them.

"They're Davey's research notebooks," said a voice that Jenkins immediately recognised, and he turned to face Professor Smythe-Brightly.

"I was just on my way to give a lecture to some very needy and demanding undergraduates, when I noticed Davey's office door was slightly open," said Smythe Brightly. "I had a feeling you might be returning," he added, before stepping forward and picking up one of the exercise books. "Davey had these specially made. That's his name printed on the front cover, written in Cantonese, apparently. He said he chose green for their covers, because it was rather more emblematic of Hong Kong, than the territory's official red and white colours. I've never been to Hong Kong, so I wouldn't know but, according to Davey, the market stalls, the trams and even the famous Star Ferry, as well as many other things besides, are all painted this particular shade of green."

"And do you also know the significance of the date that's written on the spine of each of them?" asked Jenkins.

"Yes. It's the date on which Davey made his final entry in that particular exercise book," replied Smythe-Brightly. "He would then store it away in this chest and continue recording his notes in a new one. Davey never wrote on loose leaf paper or recorded his notes on a computer. Everything went in one of these exercise books. It's yet another example of the man's unique eccentricity."

The exercise books were arranged in chronological order, with the spines pointing upwards. Jenkins could see that the most recent was dated almost three months ago. "Do you know where Professor Davey would have kept the one he had in current use?" he asked.

"Almost certainly he would have kept it with him," replied Smythe-Brightly. "A good researcher can never be sure when some useful piece of information or, original thought, will come his way. Anything Davey considered worthy of recording would go straight into his notebook, thereby ensuring it was available for future reference. If his current research notebook isn't somewhere in here or at his home then I imagine he must have had it with him, presumably in his briefcase, when he was attacked."

Yet something else that appears to have gone missing, thought Jenkins, before moving to his next question. "Did Professor Davey say anything to you about his current research? Or perhaps mention something about what he'd become involved with recently?"

Smythe-Brightly gave the matter barely a moment's thought, before gently shaking his head. "No, I don't recall him mentioning anything and it would have been extremely unusual if he had. Davey was extremely tight-lipped about such things. The first I or, for that matter, anyone else got to know what he'd been concerning himself with, was invariably when his conclusions appeared in print, either in some academic journal or in one of his many published books. Like so many other serious academics, myself included, Davey was alert to the ever present possibility of plagiarism. Sadly, there are an ever growing number of third rate, so-called academics, employed in equally inferior institutions, constantly on the look-out for other people's good work to steal and claim as their own."

Jenkins wasn't interested in Sir Peregrine's thoughts on the current scandalous state of twenty first century academia, and attempted to bring him back to the point. "So, you have no idea what it was that Professor Davey was involving himself with over recent days and weeks?"

"Essentially, no," confirmed Smythe-Brightly. "However, there was one unusual incident, a couple of weeks ago, that made me wonder what he might be concerning himself with. Quite out of the blue, he asked me to comment on some whimsical notion of his. He described it as a 'hypothetical historical constitutional matter', although I would better describe it as fanciful lore. He asked what I thought the constitutional position would have been if Charles II had fathered a legitimate child, in addition to the God knows how many illegitimate ones he sired. It was a question to which I'm sure he already knew the answer. He certainly didn't need to ask me, a constitutional expert. Nevertheless, I humoured him and told him the constitutional position was easy to describe. The child would be the rightful heir to the throne. It was as simple as that."

"Was that all?" Jenkins asked.

"Not entirely," Smythe-Brightly replied. "I asked if he had in mind James, Duke of Monmouth, a child born to Charles' mistress, Lucy Walter. At one time she was alleged to have secretly married Charles, but it's an apocryphal tale that was well and truly debunked many years ago, as Davey well knew. However, he made it clear that in the hypothetical situation he was considering, the child was a female Catholic, born to a Catholic mother who, herself, was drawn from minor French gentry. I said if that were the case, since Charles II died in 1685 and The Act of Settlement, an act prohibiting a Catholic from inheriting the throne, wasn't passed until 1701, constitutionally, nothing would have changed. And the child would still be legal heir to the throne. Politically, however, everything would have changed. And, if Charles was as intelligent and politically astute as he is generally considered to have been, then he would probably have thought it best to keep the marriage secret and hide the child away. I'm quite sure Davey knew all of this before he ever raised the subject with me. I believe he was simply seeking reassurance for a conclusion he had already come to, something I have never known him feel the need for before. Neither have I ever known him spend his time pondering over hypothetical matters."

"And that was the end of it?" enquired Jenkins.

"Well, again, not entirely," replied Smythe-Brightly. "Davey's final question was to ask what I thought the current constitutional position would be, if a direct descendant of that hypothetical child was found to be alive today, and was someone who was not a Catholic. I told him that would be a far more complicated and inevitably controversial matter. It was certainly not a question to which I could provide an immediate and straightforward answer. Indeed, such a revelation would, without doubt, have all manner of unforeseeable legal and political ramifications. I reminded Davey that the British Constitution, in so far as it exists, is an extremely piecemeal affair and certainly doesn't deal with every possible eventuality. At that point our discussion on the matter came to an end. Quite frankly, I found the whole affair extremely odd, especially since Davey was so very insistent that I shouldn't mention our conversation to anyone else."

"And have you?" asked Jenkins. "Apart from just telling me about it have you mentioned the matter to anyone else?"

Smythe-Brightly cleared his throat. "I believe I did unwittingly let reference to it slip out on one occasion.

I was enjoying dinner with an old university friend, someone who was also a contemporary of Davey's at Balliol, and he asked after him. It was on the evening of the same day that I'd spoken with Davey, so it was still very fresh in my mind. Before I realised it, I'd told my friend all about it. Too much wine I suppose! Just like me, he thought the whole episode sounded rather outré and, for Davey, very much out of character."

"Who is this friend you were having dinner with?" asked Jenkins.

Professor Smythe-Brightly again cleared his throat, before eventually giving an answer. "Sir Angus Merryweather KC. You may have heard of him. He's a very eminent jurist who, amongst many other things, is senior legal adviser to the Court of St James. We meet up for dinner from time to time, to reminisce on our student days and exchange views on topical legal and constitutional matters."

Smythe-Brightly pointed to the clock on the office wall. "I really must beg to take my leave, constable. I'd completely lost track of the time and I see that it's now less than a minute to the start of my scheduled lecture. With student fees at ten thousand a year there'll be something approaching a riot if I turn up late."

Jenkins had once been a fee paying university student himself, although not at ten thousand a year. He gave a slight shrug of resignation.

"I'll be dealing with the Laws in Wales Acts of 1535 and 1542," said Smythe-Brightly. "As a Welshman you may be interested. You're very welcome to sit in on my lecture if you wish."

Jenkins declined the invitation, before following Smythe-Brightly out into the corridor and asking him one final question. "I believe Professor Davey recently acquired an old parchment in need of some TLC. Do you have any idea where he might have taken it to have the work done?"

"Almost certainly he would have taken it to the University's Technical Services Department," responded Smythe-Brightly, as he flew down the corridor. "When you get there, just ask for Elvis Presley."

Jenkins wondered if he'd heard correctly, but it was too late to check. Smythe-Brightly had exited the corridor and disappeared out of sight.

The University's Technical Services Department is housed in its own purpose built premises. Jenkins entered the building in a state of uncertainty. Had he misheard Smythe-Brightly's instruction or was it the Professor's attempt at a rather unfunny, practical joke? Or, was there really a technician called........?

Jenkins was beginning to feel rather like a young apprentice who'd been sent to the stores to ask for a tube of elbow grease or a tin of striped paint. But he steeled himself, approached the reception desk and grasped the nettle. "Can I please speak to........Elvis Presley?" he asked somewhat hesitantly.

"I'll just see if he's available," replied the receptionist, without batting an eyelid.

Jenkins gave out a sigh of relief.

A few moments later a bespectacled, tubby, bald man of about fifty years of age appeared. Jenkins showed his police ID, before enquiring if Professor Davey had recently brought in an old parchment in need of some restoration. Elvis confirmed that indeed he had and that he was the document conservator who had carried out the required work. The Professor had brought in the parchment on the previous Monday morning, Elvis explained, and the task had been completed later that day. But it wasn't until the next day, Tuesday, when the Professor returned to collect it.

"Exactly what time on Tuesday was it?" enquired Jenkins.

"I couldn't tell you," Elvis replied. "Tuesday was my day off, so I'd passed everything over to my assistant, Miss Monroe. She should be able to tell you exactly when it was."

Elvis called out to a bespectacled, tubby little woman of about fifty – the pair could have been twins. "Marilyn, do you remember when Professor Davey collected his package?"

Elvis Presley! Marilyn Monroe! Where the hell am I? Jenkins thought to himself.

"Professor Davey called for it around ten past six on Tuesday evening," explained Marilyn. "He was very lucky to find me still here. We normally close at six. I was just about to lock up and go home when he turned up."

"Do you remember what he did with the package after you gave it to him?" asked Jenkins. "Did he open it? Or, did you see him put it straight into his briefcase, perhaps?"

Marilyn gave a shrug. "I really couldn't say. My mind was elsewhere. I was running late for my bus and just wanted to get locked up and away. I couldn't even tell you if he had a briefcase with him. All I remember is that he seemed to be in a bit of a hurry himself."

With nothing else to add, Marilyn Monroe went back to her duties and Jenkins returned to questioning Elvis Presley. "What can you remember about the text on the parchment?"

"Nothing, really," Elvis replied, "other than it was written in French, not a language I'm too familiar with. Anyway, all Professor Davey wanted me to do was clean it up a bit. You know, remove stains and make the writing more visible, that sort of thing. And I made a few copies using multispectral imaging, to make it even easier for him to read. I put everything in the package that I left for him."

As he was about to leave, Jenkins looked around the room and saw there was a CCTV camera high up in one corner. It gave him an idea. "Where's the security office?" he asked.

There were six CCTV monitors in the security office, all under the supervision of a single member of staff who was, in fact, paying them very little attention. He was clearly far more interested in what was on the screen of his smart phone than on any of the monitor screens.

The office was the hub of the University's entire CCTV system. It was where the feed from all of the University's security cameras including, most importantly, the one in the reception area of the Technical Services Department, was recorded and stored.

All recordings were retained for a minimum of ninety days. So it was possible for Jenkins to go back in time and observe Professor Davey collect the package from Marilyn Monroe, and then watch him put it straight into his briefcase. It happened at precisely ten minutes past six, just as Marilyn had said.

"Can you zoom in on the briefcase, whilst Professor Davey has it open?" Jenkins asked the security officer. "I want to see if there's anything else inside it."

The limited resolution of the resulting image was too poor to identify precisely what it was, but it was clear enough to confirm there was something else in the briefcase. Presumably the mysterious Chinese document, thought Jenkins, and maybe the Professor's research notebook as well.

Recordings from other cameras around the University confirmed that having collected the parchment Davey went directly out into the City, presumably on his way to meet with Fairfax at The Peach Tree.

Jenkins got the security officer to make him a copy of the relevant recorded extract, before asking the man's name, in case he needed to speak to him again.

"Just ask for Frank," said the security officer.

"Sinatra?" enquired Jenkins, remembering the namesakes of the other dead icons he had met recently.

"No," responded a somewhat puzzled looking security officer, "Shufflebottom."

Brazelle had only just returned from his visit to James Caulfield when the postman arrived with a small parcel.

"I'm sorry this is being delivered late, sir," said the postman. "You can see from the postmark it was posted in Oxford two days ago. And it was paid for as a Special Delivery, so it should have been delivered yesterday. Unfortunately, some idiot back at the sorting office put it in the wrong bag and it wasn't until this morning we discovered the mistake. Sorry about that. I hope it isn't something you were expecting urgently."

Brazelle assured the postman there was no need for anyone, least of all himself, to feel overly concerned. Not only had he not been expecting the package urgently, he hadn't actually been expecting it at all.

The package contained a green A4 exercise book, with a single large Chinese character on its front cover. There was also a brief note enclosed, confirming the sender was Professor Davey and explaining why he had sent it.

Enclosed is a notebook containing a record of my research findings concerning Lady Adeline Harfield. I've sent it to you after coming to the conclusion that, at least for the time being, it will be safer if it is kept in your custody than it will be in mine.

Sometime over the recent weekend, both my home and my office at the University were unlawfully entered and, it would appear, searched by a person or persons unknown. I am quite certain of it. Curiously, however, on neither occasion was anything taken, despite the presence in both places of a number of artefacts of significant value. I have, therefore, come to the very obvious conclusion that the trespasser(s) must have been searching for something very specific. Something, it would seem, they failed to find.

Had these events taken place more recently, I might have considered other possibilities but, as it stands, I have convinced myself that the enclosed notebook is the item that was being searched for. I have drawn this conclusion despite my having endeavoured to be as discreet as possible about my Harfield research.

Fortunately, when the searches of my home and office took place, the notebook was with me, safely locked away in my briefcase. But who knows what may happen in the future. Those who are prepared to commit burglary in pursuit of their aims may not give up easily and may well be prepared to carry out an even more serious criminal act, in order to achieve their objectives.

Please take good care of it, as it is the only copy that exists. I shall contact you again soon, once I have successfully dealt with another, rather more pressing, matter.

Brazelle poured himself another mug of coffee, before opening Davey's notebook and beginning to read......

It has long been believed by historians of the period that there was a secret Codicil attached to the Will of King Charles II, the contents of which were known only to the King's two executors, Monsieur Allard and Colonel John Aston. But it has also been generally assumed that, even if such a document ever did exist, it merely contained details of an especially generous bequest that was made to one or more of Charles's many mistresses or illegitimate children, and that it was kept secret, only to avoid the others from knowing they had been treated less favourably.

Discovery of Adeline's alleged memoir, however, cast an entirely new light on the matter. Whereas, previously, I had thought the hypothesised Codicil to be of no great significance, historically speaking, after hearing about Adeline's alleged memoir, I considered it to be of potentially enormous importance. Apart from the missing Bollezeele church records that could have confirmed the marriage of Charles Stuart, the baptism of Adeline and the death and burial of her mother, the Codicil is quite possibly the only other document that might support Adeline's alleged claim.

There remained the possibility, of course, that either Allard or Aston had destroyed the Codicil, after carrying out the King's instructions contained within it. But I considered such action to be highly unlikely. Experience has taught me that when a monarch or other powerful individual dies, their former loyal aides are extremely reluctant to destroy, or discard, any of their former master's documents or correspondence. It seems that such an act was frequently seen as something akin to sacrilege. Fortunately, at least from the historian's point of view, this fairly commonplace attitude has resulted in the survival of many useful documents. Some of which have later proved to be highly controversial or even, on occasion, patently incriminating, although they may not have been perceived as such at the time of their creation or preservation.

With these thoughts in mind, I began my search for the King's Codicil by first seeking out the Wills of Monsieur Allard and Colonel Aston.

Allard, a childless bachelor, was the first of the two men to die. According to his Will, which was proved at the Prerogative Court of Canterbury in late 1685, he left the bulk of his estate, including all of his personal papers, to his long time friend and colleague, Colonel John Aston.

Several months later, in March, 1686, Colonel Aston also passed away. And according to his Will, also proved at the Prerogative Court of Canterbury, he left his entire estate to his sole surviving daughter, Lucy.

One thing was now clear. If the hypothesised secret Codicil ever did exist and had survived, and there was to be any chance of locating it, then it was necessary to find out what happened to Lucy Aston.

Sunday 5th September 1686. Seven months after the completion of the building of the first Harfield mansion and six months after the death of Colonel John Aston.

The Anglican priesthood was not The Reverend Simeon Farrar's first choice of career. During the time of the English Civil War, whilst he was still a young boy, he had been stirred by tales of the exploits of Matthew Hopkins, the self-styled Witchfinder General. It had inspired him to also become a witch hunter, perhaps after serving his apprenticeship with the great man himself.

But, sadly, it was not to be. By the time Farrar came of age, the Civil War had ended and Hopkins was dead. The burning of mostly, elderly women, for no better reason than an unsightly wart on the end of their nose and ownership of either a black cat or crooked horned goat, was no longer seen as quite the respectable way of earning a living that it once was.

So Farrar turned to the priesthood, seeing it as an alternative and, perhaps, a more generally acceptable way to oppose Satan and all of his evil doings. Regrettably, however, it turned out not to be a particularly straightforward matter.

Due to an oversupply of newly qualified clerics and the exceptional longevity of those already established, Farrar found it impossible to secure a permanent incumbency immediately after his ordination into Holy Orders. For more than a decade he found himself having to settle for a series of curacies, sometimes very short lived. Until, that is, in early October 1665 he had a stroke of good luck. He was on a brief visit to Oxford when, by fortunate coincidence, he happened upon a public hanging.

"Who is the scoundrel being hanged?" Farrar enquired of a fellow onlooker.

"The Reverend Ambrose Snook," the spectator replied. "Until last month he was the vicar of Prinsted. He's said to have made a written confession to stealing church silver and being a molester of young virgins, as well as admitting to many other crimes. Some say he was in league with the Devil."

In more enlightened times, when Matthew Hopkins was still alive and following his vocation, Snook would most probably have been burned at the stake. But a hanging is better than nothing, thought Farrar, as he hot-footed it to the Bishop's mansion, there to plead to become Ambrose Snook's replacement in Prinsted.

Impressed by Farrar's professed piety and his stated desire to restore true Christian values to Prinsted, a parish that had been so wickedly served during Snook's twenty eight year tenure, the Bishop appointed him to the Living on an initial six month trial. The success or otherwise of this probationary period was to be judged, personally, by the Bishop himself.

Sadly, the very next day, after partaking of a particularly lavish luncheon, complemented with a most generous supply of red wine and much strong ale, the Bishop stumbled out of his pulpit, broke his neck and died. One consequence of this unfortunate incident was that, more than twenty years later, Farrar remained in post as the vicar of Prinsted, his six month probationary period still to be assessed.

After more than two decades of listening to The Reverend Farrar's sermons, the good folk of Prinsted were well aware of the three essential requirements to gain their place in heaven: repent of your sins; accept Jesus as your personal Lord and Saviour; and, perhaps most importantly of all, give generously to the Church.

It was the first Sunday of the month and, under normal circumstances, The Reverend Farrar would be preaching a sermon that would include mention of his three most favourite topics: the Day of Judgement; death; and, damnation. And he would quote freely from the Book of Revelation, with copious references to the four horsemen of the Apocalypse and the many and varied torments of hell.

"And on the Day of Judgement," Farrar would bellow, "there will be ceaseless weeping and much tearing of hair and gnashing of teeth........."

It was a sermon that invariably left the bald and undentured members of Farrar's congregation, of which there were a number, especially distressed.

But today would be very different.

Today, Reverend Farrar would be engaged in a far more joyous undertaking. He would be conducting a marriage ceremony. One in which the much loved and respected Prinsted doctor, Robert de Calvairac, would wed his bride, Lucy Aston.

Until the previous March, Lucy had been residing in her father's house, seventy miles to the south of Prinsted. But shortly after the Colonel's death, she had been persuaded by her close friend, Adeline, to move into the Harfield mansion. It was there that she met Dr Robert de Calvairac for the first time.

Robert had been a boyhood friend of Sir Richard Harfield, in the days when he was still known as Adam Wellings. And their friendship had resumed when Adam reappeared in Prinsted under his new identity. Quite understandably, Robert soon became a frequent visitor to Harfield House and it was there that he cast his eyes on Lucy Aston for the first time.

At the time of their first meeting, Lucy was a thirty three year old spinster and Robert was a bachelor ten years her senior. Both had reached a point in their life where they wondered if their marital state was ever likely to change. For many years past, each of them had been committed to the service of others, at some cost to themselves personally.

In the case of Robert, it had been his wholehearted dedication to the wellbeing and good health of the parishioners of Prinsted, after taking over that responsibility from his grandfather, Dr Alexander de Calvairac, whilst still a relatively young man, that had left him without time to pursue any interests of a strictly personal nature.

And for Lucy, it had been her devotion to Adeline, as she acted as her companion and helped her adapt to life in England, that at first had proved inhibiting and personally restricting. Then later, after Adeline had married and no longer required her support, Lucy had taken on the responsibility of attending to the care of her ailing father in his closing years.

To say it was love at first sight when Robert and Lucy first met would be an exaggeration. But there was definitely a spark, one that over the next few days and weeks flared into a blaze, culminating with their joint plighting of their troth.

Wednesday 19th December 1688. The day after William of Orange entered London as the victor in The Glorious Revolution. Eight days after King James II, the loser, fled to France.

The Reverend Farrar had just completed his fifteenth child baptism of the year so far. The infant was Isaac, the first son born to Robert and Lucy de Calvairac. He had been named after Sir Isaac Newton, whose seminal work, Principia, had been published by the Royal Society the previous year.

Isaac's godparents were Sir Richard and Lady Adeline Harfield, his parents' dearest friends and, by far, the wealthiest couple in the parish. Isaac was indeed a lucky child.

For the majority of those present it was a day full of joy, but for some it was one of mixed feelings. King James II had been deposed, principally because of his Catholic faith, by his protestant nephew, William, and his own protestant daughter, Mary. Richard and Adeline were reminded of the warning, voiced by Adeline's father, King Charles, in which he stated that a French born Catholic woman could never sit securely on the English throne.

All the evidence presented by current events suggested that Charles had been right. Demonstrated in very practical terms, were the lengths that a protestant dominated parliament would go, to prevent an English born Catholic male from being their Sovereign. What further lengths would they go to if the Catholic with the claim to the throne also happened to be French born and a woman? What then?

Thoughts of what could happen, if Adeline's true identity was ever discovered, prompted Sir Richard to recruit a number of retired former members of the King's Guards Regiment, the military unit he had once commanded and, without explanation, set them to work constructing a tunnel. One that led from the basement of Harfield House, to a stone built woodshed located in a thickly wooded area, more than two hundred yards away.

At the very outset of the project, each of the men was required to swear a solemn oath never to divulge to anyone the nature of the work he was undertaking. And once the tunnel was completed each man reaffirmed his oath, before returning to his home, most generously rewarded for his efforts.

Sir Richard felt that both he and his wife could now sleep a little easier in their bed. If hostile forces did ever learn of Adeline's true identity, and arrived at Harfield House as a threat to her life then, at the very least, there was now a potential means of escape.

Wednesday 30th April 1746. Two Weeks after the Battle of Culloden, in which the Jacobite forces, led by Bonnie Prince Charlie, grandson of the deposed King James II, were defeated by the forces of King George II, led by his youngest son, the Duke of Cumberland.

The longcase clock that stood in the hall of Harfield House was just striking two o'clock, as Isaac de Calvairac's eighteen year old daughter, Lucy, arrived at the front door. She had come to do something that she did every Wednesday afternoon, and many other afternoons besides, ever since the age of twelve. She had come to read to Adeline, her father's aged godmother, whose eyesight was no longer what it had once been.

Lucy had, in fact, become a frequent visitor to Harfield House from a very early age. Whilst still an infant, she would often accompany her paternal grandmother, Lucy, the person after whom she was named, on her regular visits there. And from the very beginning of their relationship, a strong bond of affection had developed between young Lucy and her grandmother's dearest friend, whom she had come to refer to as Aunt Adeline.

It was an attachment that survived and flourished long after young Lucy's mother and grandmother had both died, and she continued to call upon Adeline regularly. From Adeline's perspective, the passing of her closest friend, Lucy, had left a huge gap in her life, making young Lucy's visits all the more precious.

Adeline was in her eighty seventh year and would go on to survive for another decade. One of the perils of such longevity is the risk of outliving your spouse, your friends and even your own children. It was a fate that had already befallen Adeline. Her only child, Charles, had followed his father to the grave almost ten years earlier. Her grandson, Henry, Third Baronet Harfield, was currently the head of the Harfield household.

"What have you brought to read to me today?" Adeline asked Lucy.

"I have brought the most recent edition of the London Gazette," Lucy replied. "It has news of a battle that took place in Scotland two weeks ago. It says the Jacobite rebels were soundly defeated by the King's troops, at a place called Culloden, near Inverness. Would you like me to read the article to you?"

"I think not," said Adeline. "I would prefer to hear something of life and love, not death and conflict. Have you brought anything else?"

Lucy reached into her bag and took out three scrolled up parchments, each tied with a pink ribbon. "I brought these to show you," she said. "I found them quite by chance, just this morning. I moved a small cabinet that stood beside the bed in my late grandmother's bedroom, the room in which I now sleep, and I discovered a small lever in the wall behind. When I pressed on it, one of the wall panels came away to expose a small compartment that was previously hidden behind. Inside I found these three parchments in a box."

"Why have you brought them here?" asked Adeline.

"I thought you might help me determine what they are," replied Lucy. "They are all written in French. And, as you know, my facility with the language is somewhat lacking, despite the best efforts applied by you and my grandmother Lucy, to make it otherwise. I'm wondering if they are each some form of legal document."

"Read their titles to me," said Adeline.

Lucy did as she was asked. "Reçu de vente de terrain, Document confirmant la propriété d'un bien, et, Codicille."

"They are a land sale receipt, a document confirming property ownership and a codicil," Adeline explained.

Lucy looked bemused. "What is a codicil?" she asked.

Adeline stretched out her hand. "It's an appendix to a Will. Please pass it to me."

Although Adeline's eyesight was extremely poor, she was not completely blind. Provided the text was clear and the light was good, with the aid of a magnifying glass, she was still able to make some slow progress. But it was always a quite draining experience for her.

After handing over the parchment, Lucy kept her arm outstretched, expecting Adeline to hand it straight back. But she didn't. Instead, without saying a word, Adeline picked up her magnifying glass and with the aid of her stick walked over to the window, where she proceeded to read it.

The next ten minutes passed in silence, until Adeline eventually put down her magnifying glass and returned to sit in her armchair by the fire. But she still didn't hand back the parchment. "Have you told anyone else of your discovery? Your father perhaps?" she asked.

"No, I haven't told anyone," Lucy replied, "not even my father. He went to Oxford at first light this morning and won't return until tomorrow. There was nobody else in the house when I found them and I haven't spoken to anyone since."

Lucy was beginning to feel rather uneasy. She had never known Adeline behave this way before and found the experience rather unnerving. "Is something wrong, Aunt Adeline?" she asked.

Adeline sensed the concern in Lucy's voice and moved to reassure her. "No my dear, nothing is wrong," she said with a smile. "But tell me, have you succeeded in reading and understanding any of this parchment?"

"Not really," answered Lucy. "I saw the word Codicille written at the top and since I didn't know what that meant, I didn't bother trying to read anymore of it. I assumed it's just some rather boring old legal document that's no longer of any importance. But I thought I should make sure, before I considered disposing of it. The same applies to the other two parchments. That's why I brought them to show you."

"Well, you definitely did the right thing in bringing them here," said Adeline. "And you're also right about this parchment being a legal document, although it's certainly not a boring one. As I just explained, a Codicille is an appendix to a Will. And this particular one was an appendix to my own father's Will. One in which he bequeathed to me a substantial inheritance. I assume it must have come into your grandmother's possession, because her father was one of my father's executors, someone responsible for carrying out the terms of the Codicille. No doubt it was she who put it where you've just found it."

Adeline offered the Codicille back to Lucy. "As I recall, your grandmother left all of her personal effects to you. And it is certainly not for me to tell you what to do with a document that once belonged to her and, therefore, now belongs to you. But please believe me, Lucy dear, when I say that if it were to fall into the wrong hands, then no good would come to anyone, least of all to me and what remains of my family. How, or if, that situation may change in the future, Heaven alone knows."

Lucy hesitated in accepting back the Codicille. She suddenly felt a sense of great responsibility, a feeling she had never experienced before. And she was confused. "Why should the appendix to your father's Will create such a dire threat to you and to your family, Aunt Adeline?" she asked.

Adeline felt she had little option but to explain the truth of her origin and parentage. She illustrated her account by showing Lucy her portrait that had been painted by Sir Godfrey Kneller and the rubies that had once belonged to Queen Henrietta Maria. It was a narrative that took Adeline almost two hours to complete. And at its conclusion, she was left in a state of near exhaustion, whilst Lucy was in a state of astonishment, although not one of disbelief.

"Who else knows your secret Aunt Adeline?" asked Lucy.

"Since the death of your grandparents, there is no one outside of my family, who knows anything of what I have just told you," replied Adeline. "And I sincerely hope it continues that way. Although, who knows, perhaps the circumstances which currently make that so imperative, for the safety and well being of me and my family, may at some time in the future change for the better."

"But if secrecy is so important, why have you decided to tell me?" asked Lucy.

Adeline smiled and reached out to stroke Lucy's right arm in an act of reassurance. "Because I know you well enough to trust you with my secret, my dear and because you are currently the owner of the one document I know to still exist, that can confirm my true identity. You now have a dilemma. Do you not?"

"Indeed I do," replied Lucy. "Should I destroy it? Or, should I hide it away, just as my grandmother seems to have done?"

Adeline carried the other two parchments over to the window and, having once again picked up her magnifying glass, began to read them. "Whilst you ponder your dilemma for a while, I shall look over these two other documents that you've brought," she said.

Several minutes passed in silence before Adeline again returned to her armchair by the fire. "These documents confirm that your ancestor, Alexander de Calvairac, once owned property in La Rochelle," she said. "Perhaps, at some time in the future, if circumstances change, you or maybe one of your descendants, will be able to reclaim it. In the meantime, you may wish to store these parchments away somewhere safe, just as your grandmother appears to have done."

Lucy smiled. "And that is what I shall do, Aunt Adeline," she said.

Later that day, Lucy put all three parchments back in the box from which she had earlier taken them, returned the box to the compartment that was previously hidden behind a wall panel in her bedroom, and closed it up. Finally, she carefully removed the small lever in the wall beside the bed.

Neither Adeline nor Lucy ever mentioned the parchments again. Not to anyone. Not to their own family members and not even to each other.

Tuesday 31st January 1756. The day of Lady Adeline Harfield's burial in the Harfield family plot, within the graveyard of Prinsted Parish Church.

In her ninety eighth year, Lady Adeline Harfield passed away peacefully in her sleep, at home in Prinsted. It was Friday 27th January 1756, the same day Wolfgang Amadeus Mozart was born several hundred miles away in Salzburg.

Four days later, on the afternoon of Adeline's funeral, immediately following her burial, members of her family, together with the very few of her friends who remained alive, gathered in the drawing room of the Harfield mansion. They had come together, not just to share reminiscences of past enjoyable events in which Adeline had played a part, but also to hear the reading of her Will.

The mood of the assembly was, quite understandably, respectfully sombre, but it was not entirely devoid of optimistic anticipation.

After an hour or so had passed and the anecdotes were beginning to dry up, Mr Warbler, of Warbler, Possum and Scrote, Attorneys at Law, after taking his cue from Sir Henry, Third Baronet Harfield, announced that it was time to read lady Adeline's Will.

"This will not take long," Warbler assured the gathering. "Lady Adeline's Will is one of the shortest I have ever had to deal with. She made just two bequests." He unfurled a scrolled parchment and, to a hushed silence, began to read:

"To Lucy de Calvairac: daughter of my godson, Dr Isaac de Calvairac; and, granddaughter of my dearest friend, the late

Lucy de Calvairac, formerly Aston, I leave my rubies. Those which I wore when I married my beloved Richard and also when I sat for Sir Godfrey Kneller. Everything else, I leave to my grandson, Henry, Third Baronet Harfield."

The room remained silent as Sir Henry handed Lucy a case containing the jewellery that had once belonged to Queen Henrietta Maria. "My grandmother told me some years ago that she intended you should inherit these," he said. "And she said that you were the last woman left alive who knew of their true provenance."

The bequest came as a great surprise to Lucy. She had always admired the rubies on those rare occasions when she had seen Adeline wearing them, but she had never expected to inherit them. It also came as a surprise to at least three other women in the gathering, each of whom had.

DAY THREE – THURSDAY – CONTINUED

After leaving Frank Shufflebottom, Jenkins phoned Brazelle to tell him James Caulfield's parchment was still missing. It had disappeared, he said, along with the rest of the contents of Davey's briefcase, sometime between Tuesday evening and the next morning, when the briefcase was found empty in Charlie Rich's flat. But he made no mention of what the other contents of the briefcase might have been.

Brazelle received the call a short while after he'd received Professor Davey's research notebook and its accompanying letter. It meant he was able to provide Jenkins with some potentially useful information. First, that Davey had become convinced it was his research notebook that was the intended target of the searches of his office and home. But that the searcher(s) had clearly been unsuccessful, because the notebook was currently safe in his possession.

And second, that Professor Davey had identified James Caulfield's parchment as the Codicil that had been appended to King Charles' Will. What was written in the Codicil, however, was not yet confirmed and it would almost certainly remain that way until the Codicil was found.

Back at Oxford Police HQ, Jenkins was extremely limited in what he told DI Kershaw. He said he'd seen CCTV evidence confirming that Davey's briefcase wasn't empty when he left the University, but chose to give no further details. There were two factors restricting him in what he felt he could say, the most important of which was the undertaking he had given to Fairfax. But he was also keen to avoid making any mention of Brazelle, at least at this stage. He knew the time might very well come when, for the benefit of the investigation, he needed to reveal more, but he would only cross that bridge when, and if, he ever came to it.

The report Jenkins gave of his meeting with Fairfax, aka Snoopy, was even more heavily censored. He said only that Fairfax had called Davey's phone when he failed to show up for their planned meeting at The Peach Tree, and that a paramedic had answered and informed him that his friend was dead. At that point, aware there was nothing further he could usefully do, Fairfax had returned home.

In contrast, the news Kershaw communicated to Jenkins was entirely uncensored. It appeared to offer up a number of potentially useful leads.

First, the post mortem on Charlie Rich had confirmed that it was the bullets that killed him. But, even if they hadn't, he could not have survived much longer. The white powder seen around his mouth was heroin, and Charlie had ingested enough of it to kill a couple of fully grown elephants.

Second, the envelope discovered on the floor of Charlie Rich's flat was found to contain exactly one thousand pounds, made up of fifty used twenty pound notes. But it was the envelope itself, the only one of its kind found anywhere in the flat, rather than the money inside it that seemed to present the bigger mystery. Kershaw considered it might, potentially, provide the biggest clue(s) to solving the case. Belonging to a relatively expensive luxury brand of stationery, the envelope appeared quite out of place in Charlie's shabby, down-market abode. In addition to several of Charlie's own fingerprints, it had also yielded a single thumbprint belonging to someone of, as yet, unknown identity.

Third, the officers who'd been carrying out local enquiries had reported that, unfortunately, Charlie's neighbours had proved to be singularly unhelpful, some of them quite wilfully. But, despite that, the team had not come away entirely empty handed.

The low rise block that housed Charlie Rich's studio flat is one of three, arranged in a U formation at the end of a cul-de-sac. To the rear of the blocks is a busy railway track, separated from them by an eight foot high steel fence. A stream of varying width and depth also runs behind the blocks. Because of these obstacles, the only practical route, either to or from Charlie's studio flat, necessarily involved travelling along the cul-de-sac, regardless of mode of transport.

The investigating team very quickly discovered that, unfortunately, there were no CCTV cameras located anywhere either in or around any of the blocks. The Local Council had placed a number there in the past, but within barely twenty four hours of their installation they had all been either stolen or vandalised. DI Kershaw was understandably disappointed at the news, but, she did feel a flicker of optimism when she was told there a functioning CCTV camera not too far away, and that its recent recordings had already been requisitioned by a member of her crew.

The camera in question belonged to a scrap metal business located along the main road, just forty or so metres away from the entry into the cul-de-sac. Although principally focussed on the business's own main entrance, the camera also gave a peripheral view of the opening into the cul-de-sac. It did not have sight along its length or around the residential blocks at its far end but it did, very helpfully, capture the arrival or departure of any pedestrian or vehicle entering or exiting the cul-de-sac.

One particular twenty minute extract taken from the scrap-yard camera's recording proved to be of particular interest. The clip began, barely ten minutes after the bag-snatch had occurred, when Charlie Rich's car could be seen turning into the cul-de-sac. Presumably, he was on his way home after committing the crime.

Less than two minutes later a pedestrian, dressed entirely in dark clothing and carrying a backpack, also entered into the cul-de-sac. And fifteen minutes later the same dark figure was again seen, this time hurriedly exiting the cul-de-sac.

But it was far more than just the dark clothing and backpack that led Kershaw to conclude it was the same person who was recorded entering and exiting the cul-de-sac. There was also something unusual about the way they moved. The motion of their hips, their shoulders and their arms was all very much out of the ordinary, and quite distinctive.

And there was something else about this particular individual that Kershaw thought odd. It was an exceptionally warm evening, yet they were wearing gloves and a thick fleece with the hood up and a scarf covered the lower half of their face. It was cloudy and there was no sun, yet they were wearing sunglasses with large dark lenses. It struck Kershaw as all being quite inappropriate, unless, of course, they were attempting to conceal their identity.

A person's dress sense, of itself, is no evidence of any criminal activity, of course. But that wasn't the only factor that contributed to Kershaw's suspicion of this particular individual. The pathologist had given a one hour window as the best estimate for the time of Charlie's death. The seventeen minute gap, between Charlie's arrival home and the eventual departure of the person with the unusual gait, fitted right into it. Equally importantly, there was no one else's recorded comings and goings that did.

Finally, Kershaw shared with Jenkins what she believed was, perhaps, the most unexpected piece of news she had received that day. No fingerprints, other than the Professor's own, had been found on his pair of Blue and White Lotus Pattern Vases, the one in his office and the other in his home. But several other tiny marks found on each of them turned out to be of great significance. Their forensic analysis showed conclusively that they had all originated from the same source: an old, well used and rather grubby pair of gloves, found in Charlie Rich's flat. The discovery was more than enough to kill off any lingering notion that the robbery of Professor Davey was some random affair. It was far too much of a coincidence.

Charlie Rich was a thief. And yet it appeared that he had entered Davey's office and his home and come away without stealing anything, on either occasion. As far as both Kershaw and Jenkins were concerned, this behaviour could only be explained if Charlie was searching for something very specific and, presumably, being well rewarded for doing so.

It would also explain why Charlie was prepared to deviate so far from his usual modus operandi and carry out a street robbery. After failing to find what he was looking for in either Davey's office or his home, the Professor's briefcase was the only thing left that he hadn't searched. But what was it that he was searching for? It had to be something of value, at least to someone.

DI Kershaw knew nothing about the Chinese document, or James Caulfield's parchment, or even Professor Davey's missing research notebook. She was, therefore, at a total loss.

Jenkins, on the other hand, knew of the existence of all three of these items and, at least to his own satisfaction, had managed to eliminate two of them from consideration as the target of Charlie Rich's searches. He knew it couldn't be the Chinese document that Charlie was searching for, and not just for the reasons that Fairfax had given. At the time Charlie began his searches, it hadn't yet gone missing.

And neither did Jenkins think it was James Caulfield's parchment. At the time of Charlie's searches, apart from Professor Davey, only James and Gerald Caulfield even knew of its existence. What's more, Davey appeared to be the only one of the three of them who knew exactly what it was.

It began to look as if Professor Davey had been right all along. It really was his research notebook that was the target of Charlie's abortive searches. But who could it possibly be of interest to, and why? And where did the thousand pounds in the posh envelope found in Charlie's flat fit into the picture? From everything Jenkins had learned about the disorganised and eternally cash strapped Charlie Rich, one thing was clear, he was extremely unlikely to have been the person who stuffed exactly fifty twenty pound notes into a luxury brand envelope. It was much more likely that it was a payment made by the person who hired him to find and steal Davey's notebook, perhaps with the promise of more money to come if he was successful. If that was the case, then whoever hired him was almost certainly not the same person who killed him. Why on earth would they leave their money behind?

Jenkins began to wonder if he had perhaps been misreading the situation right from the start. A total rethink was clearly required. In the meantime, there were a couple of leads to follow up and he had a good idea where to start on at least one of them. He decided he would also take a much closer look at Charlie Rich's past criminal history and he asked to see his file.

DAY FOUR – FRIDAY

Dr Milton Fraser and Superintendent Ifor Jenkins had been friends since their undergraduate days at Cambridge. They first met on the rugby pitch, Jenkins playing on the wing and Fraser at scrum half. After graduation, when Jenkins moved to London and put on the uniform of the Met, Fraser moved to Oxford, put on a white coat and began applying his considerable intellect to the study of robotics and human anatomy, and latterly Artificial Intelligence. An extremely gifted boffin, he took his research work very seriously, although very little else.

Thinking Fraser might be able to help in the search for the suspect with the unusual gait, Jenkins paid him a visit at the research institute where he worked. He took Kershaw along with him, hoping she would not be offended by any of his rugby playing friend's jock-strap humour.

"It's great to see you again, old friend," said Fraser. "It's been a while. Remind me, when was the last time we got drunk together?"

"Christmas Eve, the year before last," replied Jenkins.

Fraser screwed up his face and gently nodded. "Ah, yes. That was the Christmas I mostly slept through. Well, one of them, anyway! I can't remember a thing about it. A great night! A truly great night!"

After introducing DI Kershaw, Jenkins explained the reason for their visit. "There are two very short videos on here that we'd like you to take a look at," he said, handing Fraser a USB flash drive. "We reckon it's almost certainly the same person who appears in both clips, mainly because of their unusual gait. We believe it's someone who can help with our enquiries into a murder case we're investigating. We're hoping you can tell us something that might help us identify who they are."

Fraser watched each of the clips several times, running them at different speeds, before making a comment. "Well, you're definitely right about the person's gait being unusual. But then so is everyone else's. No two people walk in exactly the same way, although the distinguishing features are usually far too subtle for the untrained eye to even notice, let alone explain."

"But yours is not an untrained eye, is it Milton?" said Jenkins.

"Very true," agreed Fraser with a smile. "Both of my eyes have been very expensively trained, over a number of years. So let me give you my initial assessment. The subject is female. She's probably aged in her late thirties and is approximately five feet nine inches tall. Her left leg has been amputated, most likely just below the knee, and replaced with a prosthetic. And she has suffered a serious fracture to her right shoulder that didn't heal correctly, probably due to the injury not being dealt with promptly."

To say Kershaw was dumbfounded would not be an overstatement. "You can tell all that, just from watching what's on that USB a few times?" she said. "That's amazing. I hadn't even figured out it was a woman."

"That's the difference between the trained and the untrained eye," said Fraser, rather smugly. "But we should be able to do even better than that. The way in which a person moves is not solely determined by the individual's musculoskeletal structure. The brain and the nervous system also have a part to play. Consequently, it's possible to tell a great deal about an individual's personality based on the way they walk. For example, larger upper body movement relative to that of the lower body is invariably a sign of aggression. I'm slowly getting better at understanding and interpreting such signs myself, but I'm still a total dunce compared to Amanda. Come on. I'll introduce you."

Kershaw and Jenkins followed Fraser down a windowless corridor. They passed through two locked doors along the way, each requiring both Fraser's right palm and his left retina to be scanned in order to gain entry. The second door opened into a small, sparsely furnished room. Its colour scheme was clinical white and a solitary window looked out into an enclosed empty space on the other side of the glass.

"Welcome to Amanda," said Fraser, as he waved his arms around the room. "Our Advanced Musculoskeletal And Neurological Data Analyser. Anything I can do, Amanda can do many times better. She's still a work in progress, but then she always will be, as she just keeps getting better and better at what she does."

"And what exactly is it that Amanda does?" asked Jenkins.

Fraser plugged Jenkins's USB into a slot in the wall beneath the window. "You're about to find out," he said, before calling out an instruction. "Amanda, take a look at the person on these two video clips and describe what you see."

A three dimensional holographic image of a skeleton immediately appeared in the space on the far side of the window. Jenkins and Kershaw watched as its structure was slowly altered. First, its relative dimensions were changed. Part of the lower left leg was then removed, followed by further remodelling of the bone structure, showing clear evidence of damage to the sternum and right clavicle and scapula. Finally, to complete the transformation, muscular tissue and skin were laid over the refashioned skeleton. Kershaw and Jenkins were now no longer looking at the hologram of a plain and characterless skeleton, but at a three dimensional image that could be easily mistaken for a real person.

"Amanda, in addition to what you've shown me, what else can you tell me about the subject?" Fraser enquired.

The reply came immediately. "The subject is a left-handed white skinned female, approximately 39 years of age and 175 centimetres tall. She weighs just over 51 kilograms and is therefore underweight, with a BMI of 16.7. There are clear indications that she is intelligent, rather antisocial and has a fairly aggressive and ruthless, yet loyal, personality. And she is in pain."

"Is her pain physical or psychogenic?" asked Fraser.

"Both," was Amanda's blunt reply.

"What about the subject's skeletal injuries?" asked Fraser "What can you tell me about them?"

"They were most likely acquired on the battlefield," replied Amanda.

"Thank you Amanda," said Fraser. "Now tell me the degree of confidence you have in your conclusions, expressed as a percentage."

"95.6578 percent, correct to four decimal places," Amanda replied. "Would you like me to be more precise?"

"No thank you Amanda," said Fraser. "Correct to four decimal places is just fine."

"I don't suppose Amanda can give us the subject's name and address as well, can she?" asked Kershaw.

Fraser smiled broadly. "Not yet, but, believe me, that will come .... one day."

On the way back to Oxford Police HQ, Kershaw commented on Amanda's voice. "I thought it sounded vaguely familiar," she said. "And, I don't know about you, but I found it a bit shrill."

"I thought exactly the same," agreed Jenkins. "But that's not surprising: Milton said he gave Amanda the voice of Margaret Thatcher, but the one she had before she benefitted from speech training."

Brazelle and Jenkins were not the only people to have played a significant role in bringing the Gant affair to a satisfactory conclusion. There had also been a third notable contributor – Major Daniel Coyte-Sherman of Military Intelligence. However, just like Brazelle, Coyte-Sherman had his reasons for not wishing to have his involvement made public. For him, his promotion to Lieutenant Colonel and the extra twenty thousand a year that came with it was sufficient recognition. He was perfectly content for Jenkins to stand as the lone front man for the trio's achievement.

Whoever killed Charlie Rich was clearly no stranger to the use of a firearm. So the suggestion they may have had experience on the battlefield was far from implausible. But, even if Amanda was right, whose side was the suspect on when she received her battlefield injuries? She certainly didn't have to have been serving in the British military. Jenkins was fully aware of this, but he had to start somewhere and decided it would be with Coyte-Sherman. Without mentioning anything to Kershaw, he made the call.

Jenkins repeated Amanda's description of the suspect and, almost immediately, a name came into Coyte-Sherman's mind. But he chose not to make Jenkins aware of this. Instead, he promised to make some enquiries and get back in touch.

Over the next few hours Coyte-Sherman did indeed make some enquiries. They all confirmed that his initial speculation regarding the identity of the suspect was well founded, although he didn't immediately contact Jenkins to inform him. Instead, he phoned Chris Brazelle, his one-time comrade-in-arms and a friend with whom he was well used to sharing secrets.

After explaining what Jenkins had told him, Coyte-Sherman gave Brazelle the suspect's name. "I'm as certain as I can be that it's Anna Popescu," he said. "She fits Jenkins's description perfectly. And I can't find anyone else who comes close. If it's someone who served in the British military, then it has to be her."

Brazelle was surprised. "Didn't she join a mercenary group somewhere in Africa after she was pensioned off by the Army?"

"Yes she did," Coyte-Sherman confirmed, "but it seems she returned to the UK a few months ago. I tracked her through Army pension records to get her current address. She's moved into an apartment in North London. And I've made one more discovery, Chris. She's dying. She's got a particularly aggressive form of cancer and hasn't got much time left. I guess that's why she came back home. How would you like me to play this with Ifor Jenkins?"

"For the time being, don't tell him anything," said Brazelle. "Let me have her address and I'll go and see her. We can decide what to do after that. In the meantime, if Ifor contacts you, stall him."

"Remember, Chris, Anna thinks you're dead," said Coyte-Sherman. "You'll probably freak her out if you just turn up."

Brazelle wasn't so sure. "She'll be surprised, certainly, but it would take a lot more than the sight of my ghost to cause Anna Popescu to freak out."

At the very start of the investigation DI Kershaw had given a member of her team the job of tracking Davey's final journey, mainly using recordings from various CCTV cameras the Professor had passed along his way. The officer quickly established there was no CCTV coverage of the area where the actual attack took place, but after Kershaw returned from visiting Milton Fraser, he showed her what he had managed to come up with.

There was enough in the officer's spliced together recording to confirm that Davey appeared to have taken the most direct route from the University to The Peach Tree, although there was one segment of the Professor's last journey that still remained something of a mystery. It began when he turned down Marsh Bank Lane, a narrow road along which there were no active CCTV cameras. Although it was a relatively short stretch of road, no more than a hundred metres long, it was almost fifteen minutes before the Professor reappeared, caught on a CCTV camera positioned at its far end.

It seemed unlikely that the Professor had met someone he knew and stopped for a chat. Fifteen minutes appeared to be rather a long time for a brief exchange of greetings and Davey was not known for being much of a casual conversationalist. Both Kershaw and Jenkins thought it was far more likely that he had called in somewhere. But where? And for what purpose?

Jenkins remembered seeing a reference to Marsh Bank Lane when he looked through Davey's pocket notebook. He took a second look to remind himself of the details. It was A K Houseman and Son, 54 Marsh Bank Lane. The entry in the notebook gave no clue as to the nature of Houseman's trade, so Jenkins and Kershaw got something of a surprise when they turned up at the firm's premises a short while later. It was an undertakers business.

A K Houseman and Son was a family run Funeral Directors business that had been serving the needs of the dead and the bereaved of Oxford, and the surrounding area, for the best part of a century. They were particularly proud of their reputation for excellence in the skill of embalming and their ability to make any corpse look good. The appearance of an attitude of mild contentment on the face of the lately deceased, regardless of how curmudgeonly they had been in life, came as standard. Anything else was strictly extra.

Funeral Director, Arnold Houseman, the current proprietor and manager of the business, confirmed that Professor Davey had arrived there shortly before six thirty on the previous Tuesday evening. It was not a pre-planned visit, he explained, but there was a perfectly straightforward reason for it: A K Houseman and Son were responsible for organising the funeral of the Professor's lately deceased housekeeper.

Since the Professor happened to be passing on his way to meet Fairfax at The Peach Tree, it appeared he had decided to make an impromptu visit, to view the body of his housekeeper, as she lay in an open coffin in the undertakers' Chapel of Rest.

"How long did Professor Davey stay here on Tuesday evening?" Kershaw asked.

"Oh, not long at all," replied Houseman. "I was in my office, just finishing off dealing with another client when he unexpectedly turned up. Since I was the only member of staff here, I showed him into the Chapel of Rest and returned to my office. When I came back out, about ten minutes later, he'd already returned to the reception area and was just about to leave. Sadly, that was the last time I ever saw him. His housekeeper's funeral was scheduled to take place yesterday morning, so, despite knowing by then what had happened to Professor Davey, we went ahead with it as planned."

Understandably, there were no CCTV cameras in the Chapel of Rest, but the recording from the camera in the undertaker's reception area confirmed that Houseman's suggested times for Professor Davey's arrival and departure were correct.

"What about Professor Davey himself?" Kershaw enquired. "Will you also be responsible for making the arrangements for his funeral?"

"Most certainly," replied Houseman. "Professor Davey had taken out one of our pre-paid funeral plans. It was some time ago that he provided me with very precise instructions regarding the form his funeral should take. I've been advised that the coroner will release the Professor's body on Monday. So I've already made some provisional arrangements. Unless there are any unanticipated issues to deal with, the Professor's funeral will take place at 2 pm in exactly one week's time. I shall place an announcement in the papers, both local and national, just as soon as we've claimed the body. The Professor was adamant that he wanted the minimum of fuss with the arrangements for his funeral and insisted it should take place as soon as possible after his demise, whenever that would be."

DAY FIVE – SATURDAY

Coyte-Sherman was part right. Anna Popescu did believe that Brazelle was dead. But his sudden unexpected appearance did not freak her out.

"They told me you were killed seven years ago, somewhere in the Middle East," she said.

"They lied," Brazelle responded with a grin. "I was killed in South Africa, although, as you can see, not completely. Until yesterday I thought you were dead, most likely killed by some African warlord, but possibly eaten by a lion."

"They tried," said Anna, with a faint smile. "But, as you can see, they failed. And I'm still here.....well, at least for a little while longer. How did you find me?"

"Daniel Coyte-Sherman gave me your address. He got it from Army pensions. And he tells me you've been unwell."

Anna laughed. "Unwell? That's something of an understatement. It makes it sound like I've got a mild dose of the flu! I'm dying Chris. Did Danny tell you that?"

"Yes he did. And he said you hadn't got much time left. I can't tell you how sorry I am."

"Is that why you're here?"

"In part, but it's not the only reason," Brazelle replied. "I would have still come, regardless. I have something to tell you. It seems you're a perfect match for the main suspect in a murder that happened in Oxford a few days ago. The police don't have your name yet, but they soon will. Danny and I wanted to forewarn you and perhaps see if we could help."

"Murder might not be the right word for it, Chris. Perhaps what happened to Charlie Rich could be better described as an act of justice."

"So, it was you..........Why Anna?"

Anna handed Brazelle the photograph of a young woman. "That's my one and only child. I named her Olivia. The picture was taken on her eighteenth birthday and it's the most recent one I've got of her."

"I didn't know you had any children," said Brazelle. "She's beautiful."

"WAS beautiful," said Anna. "She died from a heroin overdose almost a year ago."

"I'm sorry," said Brazelle, as he handed back the photograph. "You know, in all the time we worked together, I don't remember you ever mentioning her once."

"That's because I never did," said Anna. "Olivia was born just two days after my sixteenth birthday. Then, exactly two weeks later, I gave her up for adoption. Despite everything I've been through since, that was by far the worst day of my life. Letting her go broke my heart, but at the time it seemed like the best possible option for her. I was the daughter of a penniless single mother, a barely literate Romanian immigrant who cleaned hotel toilets for a living. And I'd left school with no qualifications. I was jobless with next to zero prospects, so what could I offer Olivia? On the other hand, her new parents could provide her with just about anything she could ever dream of. The best I could do was strike a deal. In exchange for my promise to stay out of Olivia's life and never contact her, the couple who adopted her promised to send an occasional photograph or letter, to let me know how she was getting on. The arrangement seemed to work okay for a few years, but then the photographs and the letters started arriving less frequently. Eventually, they stopped coming altogether. The photograph I just showed you was the last one I ever received. The note that came with it said Olivia had won a scholarship to Oxford and, since she was now eighteen and no longer a minor, there would be no further communication. I wasn't happy about it, but I could see the adoptive parents' point of view, so I continued to keep to my part of the original agreement. And that's when I went to Africa. It was only when I returned to the UK, just a few months ago, I found out Olivia was dead. So, I got in touch with her adoptive parents and they explained everything. Sometime during her first year at Oxford she started using drugs. To begin with it was grass. Then she progressed to cocaine and, finally, she started using heroin and crack. Eventually it killed her. And who do you think her supplier was Chris?"

"I'm guessing it was Charlie Rich," replied Brazelle.

"Got it in one," said Anna. "Charlie Rich. The man who's now seen to be far more of a victim than Olivia ever was. When Olivia died, her death barely got a mention, not even in the local press. And there was never a suggestion of anyone other than Olivia herself being to blame. The death of Charlie Rich, on the other hand, gets a mention on the TV and they describe him, rather meekly, as a petty criminal and a "low-level" dealer. But there are no LOW-LEVEL dealers, there are just dealers. They're all murderers, every single one of them. Nearly five thousand people die from a drugs overdose every year in this country. That's almost ten times the number of murders, and most of those are drugs related. I reckon I did the world a favour when I ridded it of Charlie Rich."

"When did you decide that's what you were going to do?" Brazelle asked.

"Oh, he was a dead man just as soon as I found out who he was and where he lived," Anna replied. "He had no idea who I was when I turned up at his place. To begin with he just thought I was some new client who'd come to get a fix. Then, when I pulled out a gun, he thought I was there to rip him off. So he gave me his stash. It was only when I ordered him to strip and start eating the stuff that he began to realise he had a more serious problem. I wanted him to be found just like Olivia was. Naked and dead from an overdose of drugs that he'd supplied. That's when I told him who I was and it finally dawned on him what was going to happen. Just before he could kick-off, though, I put two bullets in him. Then I shoved what was left of his stash into his open mouth."

"Did you know he'd just stolen a man's briefcase, about a mile away from where he lived?"

"No, I didn't."

"He carried the briefcase home with him. Do you remember seeing it in his studio?"

"No. The only thing I remember about his place was that it was a total dump."

"So, if you don't remember seeing a briefcase, there's no chance you took anything out of it?"

"No, of course not, why the hell would I do that? I went there to kill the guy not to rob him. He even tried offering me an envelope stuffed with cash, but I told him to stick it. Anyway, why are you so interested in this briefcase?"

"It belonged to someone I know," said Brazelle. "But never mind about that. Right now I'm far more concerned about you. What's your prognosis?"

"I've been given two months, three at most," Anna replied. "But that's what the doctors say. Me? I've got other ideas. It's my thirty ninth birthday today, which means Olivia would have been twenty three next Monday, at ten in the morning to be precise. So, I'll put some fresh flowers on her grave and then I'll call it quits."

"Is there anything I can say that might help to change your mind?" asked Brazelle.

"No, absolutely nothing," replied Anna. "My mind is already made up. I shall leave this world with a clear conscience and only two regrets. First, that I ever agreed to give up Olivia, and second, that I never got to take a bullet for you, just like you took one for me."

"It was two bullets, actually," said Brazelle, with a half smile. "But, hey, what's an extra bullet here or there between friends?"

Brazelle had done what he had originally come to do. He knew Anna well enough to know he was never going to get her to change her mind and she was becoming visibly tired.

He prepared to leave, but then a final thought came into his head. "Actually Anna," he said, "you might still be able to take a bullet for me."

DAY SIX – SUNDAY

Sir Damien Marshall could be fairly described as the quintessential senior British diplomat. Privately educated, double first from Cambridge, in a non-science subject, of course, in his case it was History and Politics, and, possession of the inevitable knighthood.

Invariably suave and self-possessed, Damien normally oozed self confidence. But not today.

Brazelle had just returned from taking the Morning Service and begun to prepare some lunch for himself when an unexpected visitor arrived.

"I'm sorry to just turn up like this," said a rather agitated Damien. "Are you alone? Rose isn't here, is she?"

"Yes, I'm alone. And, no, Rose isn't here," Brazelle replied. "She's gone out for the day with Frances."

"Yes, that's what I thought," said Damien. "And that's why I'm here. I wanted to speak to you alone, and in the strictest confidence. Is this a good time?"

"Sure, no problem," said Brazelle. "It sounds like something important. Will you be speaking to me as a future in-law or as the parish priest?"

"Both," replied Damien. "I have a confession to make and a favour to ask. And I'll get to both those things in a moment, but first I have to explain something. For the first thirty or so years of my life I believed myself to be a reasonably healthy specimen. But then something happened that caused me to reconsider my rather complacent view. There was an incident during which I suffered severe chest pains and extreme shortness of breath, soon followed by palpitations. It was unlike anything I'd ever experienced before and was quite unnerving. At one point, I thought I was having a heart attack and was about to drop dead. But, as you can clearly see, that didn't happen. As you might imagine, it prompted me to seek medical advice. But I said nothing to Frances or anyone else at the time. For all I knew it could have just been some extreme form of indigestion. But I soon found out that it wasn't. The doctors told me I was suffering from Hypertrophic Cardiomyopathy."

"All medical terms, especially those that start with 'Hyper' always sound fairly unpleasant to me," commented Brazelle. "How unappealing is this one?"

"It could be worse," said Damien. "Fortunately, mine turned out to be a relatively mild form of the malady. And, having discovered that I'd got it, I was able to take steps to mitigate its effects and make it less likely that it would kill me. In particular I had to modify my diet and avoid strenuous exercise. For the past few years I've been taking beta blockers. But there is no cure. It's a cardiovascular disease characterised by an abnormally thick heart muscle that, amongst other things, makes pumping blood around the body less efficient. The condition usually develops in young adulthood, although it can appear earlier. The medics tell me it's the most common cause of sudden unexplained death in young people, especially those who indulge in strenuous physical exercise..........And it's genetic. If a parent has it then there's a fifty percent chance that a child will inherit it."

"Well, at least that's one thing you don't have to worry about," said Brazelle. "You have no children, so you can't pass on the offending gene."

"I'm afraid that isn't altogether true," said Damien, in a faltering voice.

An awkward silence, lasting several seconds, was eventually broken by Brazelle. "Is this the confession you came here to make?"

"In part," replied Damien, "but I haven't told you who the child is yet."

There was a further brief silence, before a hesitant look of recognition appeared on Brazelle's face. "It's Rose, isn't it?"

Damien gave a gentle nod. "Yes, Chris, I'm Rose's biological father. I more or less knew it before she was even born, but I confirmed it beyond any doubt with a DNA test when she was still an infant. She doesn't know, of course, and, as far as I'm aware, neither does anyone else, least of all Frances. As you know, Frances and I became Rose's legal guardians when she was only five, after Cornelius and Justine were killed. That's meant I've been able to arrange for her to have regular medical examinations that include checking on her heart function, to see if there are any indications that she's begun to develop the condition. Thankfully there haven't been any. All the tests she's ever had so far suggest that she's got a perfectly sound heart."

"When was the last time she was tested?" Brazelle asked.

"Twelve months ago," replied Damien, "shortly before Frances and I returned from America. It was the first time Rose ever questioned the necessity for having an annual medical. But, fortunately, I eventually managed to talk her into it. I knew she'd show some resistance sooner or later. The doctors say that if no signs of the condition appear within the next few years, then it's as good as certain that Rose hasn't inherited the offending gene. So it's important she carries on having her annual check-ups, at least for a couple of years longer. I arranged for her to have the next one in a few days time, but when I mentioned it to her, she just said she'd think about it. You probably already know what that means. When Rose says she'll think about something, it invariably means she has no intention of doing it. And that's why I need your help. You're probably the only person who'll be able to persuade her to continue having the necessary checks, starting with this one."

"And if I can't persuade her, are you prepared to tell her the truth?

"Yes, of course. I know it will cause a number of other problems, but Rose's wellbeing is the most important thing."

What is it about this Harfield household, where nothing ever turns out to be exactly as it first appears? Brazelle asked himself, as he watched Damien drive away.

Brazelle knew there was evidence to suggest that up to ten percent of children were fathered by a man other than the one they believed to be their biological father. But in the Harfield household, it appeared to be a much higher percentage. It was some time ago he uncovered DNA evidence proving that Gareth Richards was fathered by Sir Cornelius Harfield and not the man whose name appeared on his Birth Certificate. He had also seen the blood group evidence that proved Sir Cornelius could not possibly be the biological father of Frances, something of which Frances herself was almost certainly unaware. And now, he'd just learned that Damien was the father of Rose.

These were far from being the only Harfield family secrets of which Brazelle had become a custodian. Honesty may very well be the best policy, or so the saying goes, but not necessarily openness. But as far as Brazelle was concerned, some secrets are best kept secret, and not always just to protect the interests of their keeper. Sometimes it can also be for the benefit of those from whom the secrets are being kept.

Maybe there were further secrets to be revealed, and more surprises to come, but one thing was now clear to Brazelle: the Harfield blood line, or at least the legitimate one, had died out with the late Sir Cornelius, the 11th Baronet. Regardless of whether Adeline's alleged claim was true or not, neither Frances nor Rose, and certainly not Gareth, had any legitimate claim to the English Throne.

DAY SEVEN – MONDAY

It was just after ten in the morning, when Coyte-Sherman phoned Jenkins to give him Anna Popescu's name, and the address of her north London apartment.

On the assumption he was dealing with an armed and dangerous cold blooded killer, Jenkins immediately called in a heavily armed SWAT team to join him in a raid on the property. But he needn't have bothered. Anna was not at home, although she had left a note saying where she would be. Jenkins was the first to read it.

"Take your team round to grave plot 570 in the local cemetery," he instructed the SWAT team commander. "According to this note, that's where you'll find her."

It was quite a lengthy note that Anna had left. And it dealt with far more than the details of her current whereabouts. It was also a suicide note and a confession to murder, although not just the murder of Charlie Rich. To Jenkins's utter astonishment, Anna also confessed to being the assassin of the MI6 traitor, Sir Ted Gant.

The bullet that killed Gant was fired from a position almost eight hundred metres away, on the top floor of an empty office block that was still under construction. The assassin was clearly an expert, because the shot was taken with a standard M24 sniper rifle, and eight hundred metres was at the very limit of its accuracy.

After the fatal shot was fired, both the rifle and the single spent shell casing were simply left where they were. To some people this might seem an odd thing for the assassin to have done, but abandoning a weapon in such circumstances is far from being unusual. At the very least, the killer avoided being caught in possession of something that could so easily tie them to a murder.

The M24 had clearly been around for a while and showed all the signs of having been well used, but it bore no serial number or any other identifying mark. Nor did it carry any fingerprints or provide any other forensic evidence. But it did possess one feature of interest. It was a left-handed model.

And one further clue was found at the shooter site. The day before Gant's assassination, some liquid plasticizer had been spilt on the concrete stairway that led up to the top floor of the unfinished building from where the fatal shot was fired. Someone had stepped in it, most likely unintentionally, and left behind a single footprint.

All of those working on the site were males who were required to wear heavy steel capped safety boots. But the size, shape and tread pattern of the footprint, clearly pointed to it having been made by a woman's training shoe, and a particularly expensive one at that.

None of this evidence had ever been made public and was presumed, therefore, to be known only to the killer and members of the investigating team. And yet, Anna had mentioned almost all of it in her letter of confession. The footprint was the only part of it to which she hadn't made any reference.

Anna also gave her reason for killing Gant. She claimed it was a matter of revenge. Retribution for his treachery that she believed had almost certainly led to the death of some of her friends and former comrades, although she gave no specific details. Revenge was also the motive she gave for killing Charlie Rich – revenge for the death of her daughter. In this case she gave very specific details, essentially repeating what she had told Brazelle.

It all sounded very convincing, especially since Coyte-Sherman had confirmed that Anna was left handed and one of the Army's best snipers. But, despite this, there remained something that Jenkins was still finding hard to come to terms with. It was all such a huge coincidence. And Jenkins was always very wary of coincidences, especially those as extreme and yet also as neat and tidy as this one appeared to be.

Kershaw was well aware that Jenkins knew more than she did about the background to the case with which they were both currently involved. That had been made very clear to her on the previous Wednesday evening, after she received her Chief's phone call putting her, at least nominally, back in charge of the investigation. She had been content to accept that situation, in the belief that Jenkins would share with her any and all evidence that was critical to solving the case. But she was now beginning to think that she had been, perhaps, a little naive in holding that belief.

Jenkins had told Kershaw about Anna Popescu, but only as the raid on her apartment was about to take place. It left Kershaw with no chance of being involved herself. And that wasn't the only incident that day that had left

Kershaw feeling side-lined and rather vexed. When Jenkins returned to Oxford, she decided it was time to confront the situation.

"How did you get to know about Anna Popescu?" she asked.

"I gave the description that AMANDA had provided to a contact I have in the Army. He came up with her name," replied Jenkins. "But he wants his identity to be kept out of all of this. He's a senior officer in Military Intelligence, so I'm sure you can understand."

"Okay, I can accept that," said Kershaw. "But you didn't need to leave it to the last minute before telling me what you were planning to do."

"Yes, you're right, I should have told you sooner, but things happened very quickly." Jenkins knew his excuse sounded extremely limp.

Kershaw handed Jenkins a note. "And there's also this. It's a message I took for you earlier today. Someone calling himself Elvis Presley and claiming to be a technician at the University phoned. He asked to speak to you, but since you weren't here he was put through to me. At first I thought he was just some weirdo nut-job, especially since he mentioned something I didn't know anything about. But he turned out to be genuine."

Jenkins read the message. It seemed Elvis had remembered one word that was written on James Caulfield's parchment. It was its heading: **Codicille**.

"Elvis Presley told me it was something Professor Davey collected on the evening he was killed," said Kershaw, "and that he probably had it in his briefcase when he left the University. He also said you knew all about it. Is that true?"

Jenkins had known from the beginning that this moment would almost certainly come at some time. It had just arrived a bit sooner than he'd hoped or anticipated. He decided to come clean, at least as far as he felt able.

"It's obvious what you're thinking," he said. "And you're right. I have held a few things back from you. Even now, though, I'm afraid I can't tell you everything. But I'll tell you as much as I can. I warn you though, it's complicated. So you'll have to bear with me, okay?"

Kershaw echoed the okay and Jenkins began his explanation.

"The day before Professor Davey was killed he came into possession of a particularly valuable document. I'm not able to tell you very much about it, except to say that it's written in Mandarin Chinese. When Davey left the University on his way to The Peach Tree, I believe he had it in his briefcase. That document is the reason I was sent here in the first place. It was my job to recover it, although I'm not the only person who wants to find it."

"Written in Mandarin?" queried Kershaw. "So, it's not the Codicille that Elvis Presley called about?"

"No, that's a seventeenth century French parchment and something quite unrelated. And neither is it what Charlie Rich was looking for when he searched Davey's office and home, and then stole the Professor's briefcase. Charlie's target appears to have been the Professor's research notebook, or at least that's what Davey himself believed. But, in any case, Charlie never found it. Davey posted it to someone he knew and trusted, and it's currently in his possession."

"My God, you weren't exaggerating when you said it was complicated," remarked Kershaw. "But how do you know all this?"

"Because the person to whom Davey sent his research notebook is a friend of mine," replied Jenkins. "And he told me. He also happens to be the same person who told me about the Codicille."

"You seem to have quite a lot of well connected friends," observed Kershaw. "Milton Fraser, some spook in Military Intelligence, and now, this mysterious individual who's got the Professor's research notebook and knows all about the Codicille. Not to mention the anonymous person with clout who sent you here in the first place. Is that the secret of your success, being well connected?"

Jenkins smiled. "I wouldn't like to think it was the whole story, but it's undoubtedly helped."

"And where does the Codicille fit into the picture?" asked Kershaw.

"When Davey left the University on the night he was killed, it's the only thing I know for sure was in his briefcase," replied Jenkins. "I saw him put it in there on a CCTV video recording. I could also see there was something else already in the briefcase when he did that – and although I can't be certain, I have good reason to believe it was the Mandarin Chinese document I was originally sent here to find. What you and I are both certain of, though, is that Davey's briefcase was very definitely empty when we found it in Charlie Rich's flat the next morning."

"So, it would appear there are two missing items. The Chinese document and the Codicille," said Kershaw. "Do you think Anna Popescu might have taken them?"

"No, I certainly don't," replied Jenkins. "Anna Popescu made her motive for killing Charlie Rich very clear in the note she left. And it all checks out. There is no reason whatever for her to have also stolen the contents of Davey's briefcase. It would make absolutely no sense. So, what are we left with?"

Kershaw made a suggestion. "After Anna Popescu left, someone else could have entered Charlie's flat and stolen what was in Davey's briefcase."

"Okay, let's examine that possibility a bit, shall we?" responded Jenkins. "If it was someone seeking the Chinese document, why would they also take the Codicille, something totally unrelated? And, conversely, if they were after the Codicille, why would they also take the Chinese document? Finally, if they were just some common thief, why on earth would they take two documents that they probably couldn't even understand, and yet still leave behind an envelope stuffed with a thousand pounds in cash, something they could not possibly have failed to notice? I think we're left with only one other possibility. Don't you?"

Kershaw nodded. "Yes. The briefcase had to be empty when Charlie Rich stole it?"

Jenkins and Kershaw took a second look at the spliced together video of Professor Davey's final journey. This time though, they zoomed in slightly on the figure of the Professor and ran the tape more slowly than before, at a little under half speed. It led to them noticing something they had both failed to spot on their first viewing, when they were primarily concerned with confirming the route the Professor had taken on his way to The Peach Tree. Professor Davey had very briefly, and rather subtly, glanced back over his shoulder, twice in quick succession, immediately prior to him disappearing out of sight down Marsh Bank Lane.

These actions could, of course, be interpreted as a sign that Professor Davey was concerned that he might be being followed. Under the circumstances, especially given what he was believed to be carrying in his briefcase, this was perhaps not too surprising. And given what happened a short while later on that evening, it was indeed highly probable that he was indeed being followed. But this was a detail that neither Kershaw nor Jenkins felt added anything to what they already knew about Professor Davey's last journey.

However, there was something else that Jenkins and Kershaw now noticed, something that hadn't previously registered with either of them. And it was a detail they both thought could be very significant. On the first part of his journey, prior to turning into Marsh Bank Lane, Professor Davey would occasionally transfer his briefcase from one hand to the other, but throughout the second part of his journey, after he'd exited from Marsh Bank Lane, he always carried it in his right hand. Why was that?

"Imagine you're Professor Davey for a moment, DI Kershaw," suggested Jenkins. "You're someone who, until now, has been living a fairly sheltered academic life. But then suddenly, you find yourself thrust into a situation fraught with intrigue and danger. In your briefcase you have something that some very ruthless people are eager to obtain, but it must not be allowed to fall into their hands. And you've begun to fear that you might be being followed, but you have no idea who you can trust. You're entirely on your own. So............what do you do?"

"If I got the opportunity, I'd probably try and hide the contents of my briefcase. Put them somewhere safe," replied Kershaw.

"I agree," said Jenkins. "I think we need to pay a second visit to A K Houseman and Son. Don't you?"

Houseman's previously given account of Davey's unscheduled visit to his business premises had suggested nothing unusual or out of the ordinary. But circumstances had now changed. New information had come to light, leading Kershaw and Jenkins to return and probe a little deeper.

The first thing they wished to establish was Houseman's assessment of Davey's demeanour, when he unexpectedly arrived at the funeral parlour.

"Did the Professor appear relaxed and at ease? Or, did he seem to be perturbed or agitated in anyway?" Jenkins asked.

"Well, yes, perhaps he did seem rather on edge when he first arrived," Houseman explained. "But given the nature of our business, it's not entirely uncommon for clients to seem a little unsettled or, sometimes, even appear quite emotional. By the time he left, though, he seemed much more at ease."

"Did you have much of a conversation with him?" asked Kershaw. "Can you remember anything of what passed between the two of you?"

"Actually there was very little opportunity for conversation between us," said Houseman. "As I told you on your previous visit, when Professor Davey unexpectedly arrived I was busy with another client. The Professor just asked if he could view the body of his housekeeper, so I unlocked the door to the Chapel of Rest to let him in and then returned straightaway to my office. Our only other, equally brief, exchange took place just before he left. He just said he intended to pay one final visit to view the body, first thing the following morning. And he asked me not to seal the coffin until after he'd been. Then he left. Sadly, of course, he never did return."

"Is it usual for someone who's lost a close friend or relative to pay two visits in quick succession to view the body?" Jenkins asked.

"It's certainly not a common occurrence, but it's not entirely unheard of," replied Houseman. "However, Professor Davey had already viewed his housekeeper's body a few days previously, so his planned visit for the next day would have been his third viewing. And that is rather more unusual."

"Is it possible that Professor Davey could have entered any other room in these premises?" asked Kershaw.

"No, certainly not on that occasion," replied Houseman. "Every room, except for the Chapel of Rest and my own office, was locked. Even the toilets were locked."

Jenkins had already been involved in one exhumation in his career. For a few moments he thought he might have to become involved in a second. But he was quickly put right on the matter. Davey's recently deceased housekeeper had not been buried, Houseman explained, she had been cremated.

It had become fairly clear what Davey had done. And, at the time he did it, it must have seemed to him to be a wise move. How was he to know that he wouldn't be in a position to return, and retrieve the contents of his briefcase from his late housekeeper's coffin the next morning?

The Chapel of Rest was searched, of course, just to be sure, but neither Kershaw nor Jenkins held out much hope that anything would be found. They were right.

Jenkins was left with the unenviable task of having to tell both Fairfax and Brazelle that the document, in which each of them was interested, was gone, quite literally, up in smoke. He was surprised by each of their seemingly relaxed responses to the news.

"You did your best, Superintendent Jenkins," said Fairfax. "I doubt anyone could have done more."

"I'm glad you see it that way," Jenkins responded, "and I'm also surprised. You don't appear to be as disappointed as I thought you would be."

"In order to thwart an enemy's plans it isn't always necessary to know what those plans are," said Fairfax. "Often, it's enough to have them just think that you do. Our intelligence tells us the Chinese have already scrapped their original plans, as they would have appeared in the missing document, and gone back to the drawing board, so to speak. Levels of signals traffic are also now back to normal. We know that the Chinese tracked down Li Yibo's son a couple of days ago. And they managed to spirit him away, back to China, before we could intervene. I think we can safely assume that he would have almost immediately told them he passed the document to Davey. They will conclude that we now have it. It would have been nice to have recovered the document, of course, but by now it would only be of marginal academic interest."

"And are you still unable to tell me anything more about this document?" asked Jenkins.

"Afraid so, old boy," replied Fairfax. "But trust me, it would probably only give you sleepless nights if I did."

"And where does this now leave me?" asked Jenkins.

"That's entirely up to you," replied Fairfax. "Neither Naval Intelligence or any of the other intelligence services have any further interest in the Davey case. However, if you wish to remain involved yourself, then that can be arranged. Is that what you want?"

"Yes. I'd like to see this case through to a final conclusion," Jenkins confirmed. "If nothing else, there's still the identity of the person who hired Charlie Rich to be discovered. I'm extremely curious to know why they did."

Brazelle's reaction to the news that the Codicil had been destroyed was also far more relaxed than Jenkins had expected. He was keen to know why.

"Since we last spoke on the matter, I've learnt something that's made a significant difference to the way I think about the Codicil," Brazelle explained. "I won't go into detail, and you may think it an odd thing for me to say, but, quite frankly, maybe the Codicil's destruction, before anyone had a chance to actually read it is the best thing that could have happened."

"Well, you're certainly right about one thing," said Jenkins. "I do think it's an odd thing for you to say. After all, without the Codicil you'll probably never know for certain whether or not Adeline really was who she allegedly claimed to be."

"And, all things considered, maybe that's a good thing," responded Brazelle. "Sometimes, uncovering an old truth can be extremely disruptive to the peace and tranquillity of the here and now. I've reached the conclusion that would almost certainly be true in the case of the Codicil. Even before you brought this news, I'd already decided that it was best to let sleeping dogs lie. Whether it was true or not, Sir Cornelius was almost certainly the last of the Harfield family to know the whole of Adeline's alleged story. And, if I have anything to do with it, that's how it will remain."

DAY EIGHT – TUESDAY

Jenkins arrived for dinner at Harfield House shortly before seven. He was looking forward to spending an evening during which he could forget about his day job for a while.

Rose, however, had other ideas and Jenkins had barely crossed the threshold before she began her interrogation. "Chris tells me you've been working on a couple of cases in Oxford. How are things working out?"

"Very well, as it happens, or so it would seem," replied Jenkins. "We've identified an offender in both cases."

"And you've arrested them?" asked Rose.

Jenkins shook his head. "No. That hasn't been possible. And there won't be a trial either. Both offenders are dead, and you can't prosecute a dead person. As it turned out, offender number two killed offender number one and then committed suicide a few days later. We have to produce a report for the coroner, of course. But once that's done, there'll just be a couple of inquests and then both their cases will be closed. Having said that, though, I'm still left with a couple of loose ends to clear up, but hopefully they shouldn't take too long to get sorted."

"What will you do then?" asked Rose. "Will you return to London and get back to searching for Ted Gant's killer?"

"Well, I might be returning to the Met, although that's not yet certain. But I definitely won't be going back to searching for Gant's assassin. As far as the Met is concerned that case is also just about to be closed. Gant's killer has been identified."

Rose looked surprised. "You've caught Gant's killer? Is that for definite?"

"Well it certainly seems that way," said Jenkins, before looking at his watch. "The Met Commissioner is giving a press conference in about an hour. So you'll be able to get his take on the case on the TV news later tonight. It's sure to be all over tomorrow's papers."

Rose appeared bemused, anxious almost. "And you're quite certain you've got the right person?"

Jenkins thought it an odd question for Rose to ask, but it was the intonation in her voice he found most surprising. It suggested disbelief. "Well, a lot of people would be surprised if it turned out we've got the WRONG person," he said. "The evidence pointing to their guilt is really quite considerable. For a start, they wrote a letter confessing to being the assassin. In it they mentioned facts about Gant's shooting that have never been made public. Stuff that only members of the investigating team and the killer should know. But that's not all. Whoever made the shot that killed Gant had to be an expert sniper, most likely someone who'd had military training and experience. And there was other evidence that pointed to the killer being a left-handed female. Our candidate fits that profile perfectly."

Rose was still looking puzzled. "Who is this woman?" she asked.

"Her name is Anna Popescu," replied Jenkins. "Until a few years ago she was a warrant officer in the British Army. But she was pensioned off after losing much of her left leg in a landmine explosion. And it wasn't the first time she'd been wounded in the line of duty. From all accounts she was quite a star. We've been told she was one of the Army's deadliest snipers and one of the first females to serve with Special Forces. It's a very sad way for her life to have ended."

"You mean she's dead?" queried Rose.

"Yes," replied Jenkins. "She's the same person I referred to as offender number two a few moments ago. She shot herself a few days after killing a drug dealer called Charlie Rich. In the note she left, she confessed to both murders and explained her motive behind each of them."

"And what was her motive?" asked Rose.

"Revenge," replied Jenkins, "in both cases."

Brazelle decided that Rose's interrogation of Jenkins had gone on long enough. "When Ifor accepted our invitation to dinner, Rose, I'm quite certain he didn't suspect it included a session with the Spanish Inquisition."

Rose got the message and her bemused look changed into a smile. "Absolutely!" she said. "My apologies for getting a bit carried away with the cross-examination. I'll leave you two to talk about something else for a while, whilst I visit the kitchen and give Mrs Richards a hand preparing dinner."

Left alone with Jenkins, Brazelle posed a question of his own. "You've probably already guessed that I knew Anna Popescu, haven't you?"

"I didn't know for certain, but, given the business the two of you used to be in, I thought it highly unlikely that your paths hadn't crossed at some time. I imagine you also know quite a lot more than is generally known about Gant's assassination. All of it learned from Daniel Coyte-Sherman I suspect. He was involved in the early stages of the investigation and, knowing how close the two of you are, I can't believe he hasn't talked to you about it."

Brazelle smiled. "You're right. He did. But while we're still alone perhaps you can tell me what you really think about Gant's assassination. Despite everything I just heard you tell Rose, I still get the feeling you aren't totally convinced that Anna Popescu is the killer."

"That's probably because I'm not," replied Jenkins. "In the case of Charlie Rich, I'm absolutely sure she did it. Everything she wrote in her confession checks out one hundred percent. And we have CCTV evidence to back it up but, in the case of Gant? The Commissioner and the rest of the investigating team may be convinced, but me? I'm not so sure."

"And why is that?" asked Brazelle.

"Well, for a start, I'm not entirely persuaded that Anna Popescu was even physically capable of carrying out the assassination. She was diagnosed with terminal cancer just over six months ago and she's been having chemotherapy, on and off, ever since. She had the last session just the day before Gant was killed and, according to her oncologist, it really knocked her for six. The way he described the physical state it left her in, it's hard to see how she could have possibly climbed up sixteen flights of stairs the very next morning, especially whilst carrying a sixteen pound M24, and then, immediately after the shooting, made a quick getaway."

"But you didn't know Anna," said Brazelle. "The Anna Popescu I knew was tough, extremely tough. If she had a mission to accomplish, there was very little that could prevent her from seeing it through."

"And just how well did you know her?"

"Well enough to take a couple of bullets for her."

"Okay, so suppose she was able to get up the stairs," suggested Jenkins, "that's not the only thing that gives me doubts. There was also a footprint we found close to the firing position. Its size and shape match Anna's non-prosthetic right foot reasonably well, but its tread pattern's given me a bit of a headache. It belongs to a type of training shoe that normally sells for around five hundred pounds a pair. When we searched Anna's apartment, not only did we fail to find any trainers that matched, we didn't find any trainers at all, just boots, six pairs of them. And none of them cost more than a hundred quid a pair. Now do you see my problem, Chris?"

Although Coyte-Sherman had told Brazelle everything he'd learned during the early stages of the investigation into Gant's assassination, it was only sometime later that the evidence presented by the footprint's tread came to light.

So Brazelle was unaware of it. In the end, though, did it really matter? There was all the other evidence pointing to Anna's guilt. The mystery of the relatively expensive trainers didn't cancel out any of it.

"Well you obviously see the footprint as a problem," said Brazelle. "But what do the rest of the investigating team and the Commissioner think about this training shoe conundrum?"

"The rest of the team don't seem to see it as much of an issue at all," Jenkins replied. "They reckon Anna probably got rid of the trainers soon after killing Gant, when she realised she might have left a foot print behind, but before she decided to confess to the killing. The trainers' price tag doesn't seem to concern them at all. Not like it bothers me. And as for the Commissioner, well, he's been under such enormous political pressure to get a result, I reckon he'll go for almost anything that looks reasonably plausible, just to bring the whole thing to an end."

"So, if you don't believe Anna killed Gant, why do you think she wrote the letter confessing to it?" asked Brazelle.

"Oh, come on Chris, you can do better than that. It was because she was covering for someone else of course."

"Like who?"

"Like someone she owed a big favour, perhaps someone who once took a couple of bullets for her."

Brazelle smiled. "Now it's your turn to do better, Ifor. I have a cast iron alibi for the day Gant was killed. And you know it. But, in any case, I'm neither left-handed nor a female. And I take a size eleven shoe and have never worn expensive trainers in my life."

"I've never thought it was you, Chris. And I still don't. But you didn't seem in the least bit surprised when I mentioned Anna Popescu's name earlier. I assume Daniel told you she was a suspect for the murder of Charlie Rich, but he knew nothing about any connection between her and Gant's assassination. So why didn't you appear surprised when I mentioned it?"

"Because I already knew," said Brazelle. "Daniel contacted me just after you first got in touch with him. He'd guessed straight away that the person you were looking for was probably Anna. But he didn't want to give you her name until he was absolutely certain. So he called me and I paid her a visit. That's when she told me what she'd done. And what she planned to do."

"Did that include telling you she intended to take her own life?"

Brazelle hesitated slightly before answering. "Yes it did. She even told me where, how and when she was going to do it. And I didn't try to talk her out of it."

"Why not?" asked Jenkins.

"Two reasons," replied Brazelle. "For one thing I knew it would be pointless to even try. But, more importantly, I could tell she was suffering, both physically and mentally, and I knew it was only going to get worse. What would I have achieved if I'd been successful? Leave her to linger in pain for a few more weeks until the inevitable eventually happened? I may be a priest, but I'm also her friend who could do nothing to ease her pain. As you well know, Ifor, life doesn't always throw up easy options for us to choose between. We live in an imperfect world. Sometimes the choice we're given is between something bad and something even worse. With Anna Popescu I was faced with one of those situations."

Brazelle poured himself another whisky and topped up Jenkins's glass. "Whilst we still have a couple of minutes before Rose returns, let me change the subject and ask you a question. You said earlier that you still had a couple of loose ends to tie up. Can you tell me what they are?"

"Sure," Jenkins replied. "First, I want to nail the person who hired Charlie Rich, someone complicit in a conspiracy to commit robbery, one that ended up with the victim being killed. And, second, I want to find out who really did kill Ted Gant."

DAY NINE – WEDNESDAY

Jenkins spent a good deal of the morning reading through Charlie Rich's considerable criminal file. Since Charlie's lawbreaking career stretched back more than thirty years, to when he was in his early teens, there was a lot to get through.

It was just past mid day when Kershaw brought him a mug of coffee and enquired if he was hungry.

"I'm starving," said Jenkins.

"And how do you feel about Italian food?" asked Kershaw.

Jenkins licked his upper lip. "I absolutely love it."

Kershaw smiled and handed him a Garibaldi biscuit.

"You're too kind," said Jenkins, with obvious disappointment.

"So I've been told," responded Kershaw with a broad grin. "I thought it might sweeten the taste of having to read through that lot. What exactly are you hoping to find?"

Jenkins took a sip of his coffee and a bite of his Garibaldi biscuit. "I don't really know. Some kind of revelation hopefully, but, at the very least, some inspiration. I think it's more than likely Charlie was hired by someone with whom he already had a connection, perhaps someone from his criminal past. I've been going through his file in reverse chronological order, hoping that at some point, something, perhaps a name, would leap out at me. I've already worked my way back to when Charlie was just about to turn eighteen, but so far no such luck. Having gone this far, though, I might as well see the job through to the bitter end. What about you, have you had any luck identifying who the fingerprint on the cash filled envelope belongs to?"

"Not so far," replied Kershaw, "but we think we've managed to identify just about all the retailers who sell that particular brand of envelope. It turns out there are only a couple of dozen, mostly dotted around London. I've got someone checking to see if any of them keep customer lists. What did you think of your Italian food, by the way? Do you think you could manage a little more?"

Jenkins nodded and held out his hand and Kershaw passed him the remains of the packet of Garibaldi biscuits, before leaving him alone to finish reading through Charlie's file.

A further hour passed, and Jenkins had got all the way back to the very earliest days of Charlie's criminal career. With nothing tangible to show for his efforts so far, he was beginning to feel he'd been wasting his time, when a name did eventually leap off the page. A big smile came across his face as he leaned back in his chair.

"Got you," he said to himself.

DAY ELEVEN – FRIDAY

Despite the short notice given of Professor Davey's funeral, it still turned out to be a relatively well attended event. There were no family members present, not even a distant cousin or two, but there were a significant number of the Professor's friends and colleagues, both past and present, and at least a few dozen of his students. Although most of those in attendance were people drawn from the world of academia, there were quite a few who weren't. Superintendent Ifor Jenkins and The Reverend Chris Brazelle, for example, were also present.

"I was wondering if you'd turn up," said Jenkins, "especially since you said you hardly knew the man."

"It's true we weren't particularly well acquainted, but we appear to have ended up having quite a strong connection," responded Brazelle. "I can't help thinking that if I hadn't gone to see him about Lady Adeline's alleged claim, and he hadn't decided to research the matter, he might still be alive."

"Does that mean you feel in some way responsible for his death?" asked Jenkins.

"No, absolutely not," replied Brazelle. "The Professor's death is entirely the responsibility of Charlie Rich and whoever hired him to steal his research notebook. I'm merely what might be described as a bit part player in the tragedy."

The funeral was certainly not a religious affair. There were no hymns or prayers. And the Celebrant who took charge of proceedings, and who was certainly no priest, admitted at the outset that he had never actually met Professor Davey. His role, he said, was not to give a eulogy, filled with anecdotes and personal recollections of the deceased, but to ensure the Professor's clearly expressed wishes, as to the form his funeral should take, would be fully complied with.

A couple of recorded songs and two poems later, one of each in Cornish, with the others in Cantonese, and the committal curtain was closed, bringing the formal proceedings to an end. All that remained was the funeral wake, which was to be held at the late Professor's favourite eatery, The Celestial Gardens Chinese Bar and Restaurant.

"What do you intend to do now?" Jenkins asked Brazelle, as the pair filed out of the Crematorium Chapel with the other mourners. "Will you be coming to the Celestial Gardens?"

"No, I've done what I came to do and paid my respects," replied Brazelle. "By the sound of it, though, you intend going along there."

"Yes, I'll be going," confirmed Jenkins. "Unlike you, I haven't yet done everything I came here to do. But it shouldn't take too long before I have."

Jenkins was one of the last to arrive at the Celestial Gardens. He entered into a room that was almost entirely filled by strangers. But there were two men present who he did recognise. And, given what Professor Sir Peregrine

Smythe-Brightly and Commander Algernon St John Fairfax had each said of the other, just a few days earlier, what he saw surprised and also amused him. It was a classic example of two-faced hypocrisy, he thought. The two men appeared to be quite relaxed in each other's company, behaving just as if they were the oldest and closest of friends. The pair were standing together, each holding a half empty wine glass, in discussion with a third man, someone who Jenkins had never previously met. But he knew who he was.

Jenkins went over and interrupted the group. "Good afternoon, Sir Peregrine," he said, "and also to you Commander Fairfax." To the third man he simply gave a half smile and a gentle nod.

"I thought it possible that you would attend, constable," said Smythe-Brightly. "And I see you already know Commander Fairfax. I assume you tracked him down after I identified him as Snoopy."

"Yes I did," Jenkins responded, before turning directly towards Fairfax with a big grin on his face. "And he told me what good friends the two of you are."

Fairfax glowered. "Yes indeed. It's very nice to meet you again, CONSTABLE. Just a pity it's under such sad circumstances."

Smythe-Brightly attempted to introduce Jenkins to the third member of the group. "This is one of the police officers responsible for identifying Davey's killer, Angus," he said. "My apologies constable, but I'm afraid I can't remember your name."

"It's SUPERINTENDENT Jenkins."

"Ah yes, of course, Superintendent Jenkins," repeated Smythe-Brightly, before completing the introduction of the third man. "And this is Sir Angus Merryweather. The three of us were all undergraduates together with Davey at Balliol, more than thirty years ago. We were just reminiscing on our student days, punting on the Isis and such. They were happy days indeed and, sadly, quite a contrast with today."

"Was your experience of punting on the Isis what first got you to consider joining the Royal Navy, Commander Fairfax?" Jenkins asked, mischievously.

Fairfax was not amused. "A punt is an unstable wooden crate, not a ship. And the Isis is a shallow, narrow stream, not the open sea. I think you can draw your own conclusions about that, CONSTABLE."

"I imagine Davey's case is now closed, superintendent," said Merryweather, "now that you've identified his killer. He was a petty career criminal, I understand."

"Well, you're right about Professor Davey's killer having been identified," agreed Jenkins. "And yes, he was a petty career criminal. His name is Charlie Rich and, as I'm sure you've heard, he's also now dead. So he won't be making any statements or standing trial in a court of law. But the case is far from being closed. Before that happens, I'm determined to identify the person who hired Charlie. When I do, at the very least, they'll be charged with conspiracy to commit robbery."

"Good Lord, I had no idea this Rich chap had an accomplice," said Smythe-Brightly. "I don't remember that being mentioned in any of the news reports I've seen or heard."

"It wouldn't have been," responded Jenkins, "because we haven't yet released that information to the media. The person I'm aiming to identify is far more than just an accomplice. They're the instigator of the whole conspiracy. In fact they were Charlie Rich's employer."

"Do you have any leads that might help you identify this miscreant?" asked Merryweather.

Jenkins smiled. "Yes, we do have a couple of leads. But, later today, I'm hoping to get some news that will allow me to very quickly bring the matter to a satisfactory conclusion."

Jason, one of the Chinese barmen, came over with a tray full of drinks. Jenkins was the only one not to put down an empty glass and pick up a fresh one.

"Not drinking?" enquired Fairfax.

"I never drink when I'm on duty," replied Jenkins, before taking his leave of the trio and quickly following Jason over to the bar. A few minutes later he left the Celestial Gardens and went directly to Oxford Police's forensic science department. He took with him a plastic evidence bag containing an empty wineglass.

"Check this glass for fingerprints," he instructed one of the forensic science technicians. "Compare any that you find on it to the one found on the envelope in Charlie Rich's flat. Please do it as quickly as you can. I'll wait for the results."

While he waited for the technician to report back, Jenkins phoned Kershaw and told her what he had done, and what he intended to do if the fingerprints matched up, as he believed they would. It gave her the opportunity to become directly involved in what appeared to be a critical phase of the investigation.

Less than thirty minutes later the result that Jenkins had been expecting and was hoping for was confirmed. Whoever had been holding the wineglass had also handled the envelope found in Charlie Rich's flat.

He immediately returned to the Celestial Gardens, hoping that the three men he'd been talking with earlier were all still there. Fortunately they were. And they were certainly surprised to see him reappear, especially since he hadn't come alone. This time he was accompanied by DI Kershaw and two uniformed officers, and his attitude appeared to be far less casual than before.

"When I spoke with the three of you earlier, you were all drinking wine," said Jenkins. "But only one of you was drinking red. I believe that man is the same person who paid Charlie Rich to rob Professor Davey. That makes him the person ultimately responsible for Professor Davey's death, the reason why we're all here right now. I think it's highly appropriate that what I'm about to do, I'll be doing here.....................Sir Angus Merryweather, I am arresting you on suspicion of conspiracy to commit robbery."

"Good Lord, what the hell do you think you're doing?" screamed out Fairfax as Jenkins continued to read Merryweather his rights, "Don't you know who this man is?"

"Yes, of course we do," said Kershaw. "That's why he's the person being arrested."

Merryweather raised his right hand in a gesture intended to stop any further objection to what was happening. "I'm afraid the officer is right," he said. "It was never intended to end the way that it did. But, sadly, it did. And I shall now have to face the consequences."

Fairfax and Smythe-Brightly were left speechless. They watched in silence as the two uniformed police officers escorted Sir Angus Merryweather out of the Celestial Gardens. As more of those present started to realise what was happening, the noise level in the room was reduced to barely a murmur and almost immediately people began to leave.

Jason came over with a fresh tray full of drinks and, this time, Jenkins took one. He also passed one to Kershaw.

"I thought you didn't drink on duty," said Fairfax, having recovered his composure.

"I don't. And neither does DI Kershaw," Jenkins confirmed, "but we've both been off duty for the past......" He looked at his watch, "Oh, all of twenty seconds, I'd say."

"It seems the Prime Minister was right about you, after all, Superintendent Jenkins," said Fairfax. "If you can find a spare few minutes sometime, perhaps you'll be good enough to give me a call and explain all of this. But please leave it a couple of days before you do, I think I need a little time to recover." Then, turning to Smythe-Brightly, he added: "Come on Perry, let's get a taxi up to The Peach Tree and have a T Bone. It was one of Davey's favourites and what he would have wanted."

As Fairfax and Smythe-Brightly departed, so did the rest of the gathering. Very soon, apart from the staff, Kershaw and Jenkins were the only people who remained.

"I get the very distinct feeling that you and Commander Fairfax, aka Snoopy, are more than just passing acquaintances," said Kershaw. "And, that reference to the Prime Minister? What the heck was that about? I was right, wasn't I? You really do have some friends in high places? Any chance you'll share one or two of them? Or at least tell me how to make a few for myself?"

"It's all a matter of coincidence," Jenkins replied. "Being in the WRONG place, but at the right time, and then managing to come out of the situation alive and in more or less one piece. Believe me, there is no magic formula."

"Well there is something I can recommend." said Kershaw. "And I think you've earned it."

"Jason," she called out to the barman, "let me have two large glasses of biajiu."

DAY TWELVE – SATURDAY

Having successfully identified the person who employed Charlie Rich, to search for and steal Professor Davey's research notebook, Jenkins was hoping to spend a weekend doing something other than police work. But he was going to be disappointed. Shortly after 9am he received a call telling him that Sir Angus Merryweather, who was currently occupying a cell at Oxford Police HQ, had asked to speak with him.

After his arrest, Sir Angus had admitted paying Charlie Rich to enter and search Professor Davey's home and office. But he denied having any prior knowledge of the incident in which Davey was killed and his briefcase was stolen. He claimed that Charlie must have decided to carry out the street robbery acting on his own initiative. And he'd refused to confirm what it was that he'd paid Charlie Rich to go searching for, or explain his motives for doing so. He said he would only divulge that information to Superintendent Jenkins, and asked to meet with him alone in his cell.

As now a self confessed criminal, Merryweather knew his distinguished legal career was at an end. Not only was he about to be publicly named and shamed but, just as soon as the necessary formalities were completed, he would be stripped of his status as a King's Counsel and expelled from the Bar. It amounted to a tremendous fall from grace.

Although he had been genuinely ignorant of Charlie Rich's plan to carry out the street robbery, Sir Angus still felt in some way responsible for the death of Professor Davey, a man with whom he had shared a friendship for over thirty years. That only added to his grief. It was no wonder Jenkins came upon a somewhat dispirited soul when he entered Sir Angus's cell. He couldn't help but feel a degree of pity for the man.

"I'm very grateful that you agreed to come and meet with me, Superintendent Jenkins," said Merryweather, as he forced a faint smile. "Amongst other things, it gives me the opportunity to impress upon you that I never meant for any harm to come to Davey. And I made it abundantly clear to Charlie Rich that he must not take anything other than the single item I had paid him to bring to me. Although Davey and I were very different creatures, I always considered him to be a friend. And if I had known Charlie Rich planned to commit a street robbery, I would have very definitely stopped him. It was certainly never meant to end like this."

"I'm sure it wasn't," said Jenkins. "But I'm very keen to find out why it did."

Merryweather gently nodded. "And so you shall, superintendent. But before we come to that, I was hoping you'd be kind enough to satisfy my curiosity, by telling me how you first came to suspect that I might be the person who hired Charlie Rich."

Jenkins sighed and looked at his watch. He could sense his Saturday morning being frittered away. "Once I came to realise it was Professor Davey's research notebook that

Charlie Rich was searching for, I figured he must have been employed by someone who knew about the Professor's particular way of keeping records. Then later, when I was looking through Charlie's file, I discovered that you'd been his brief during the early years of his criminal career. That's when you became my number one suspect. I guess he must have been one of your earliest clients."

"He was, in fact, my very first client," said Merryweather. "A teenage Charlie Rich was the first person I ever represented in a criminal court. And, as luck would have it, it was also the very first case that I won. Although Charlie was very clearly guilty, I managed to get the case against him dismissed on some purely technical grounds. I represented him a few more times over the next couple of years, although my advocacy didn't always prove to be more persuasive than the mountain of evidence pointing to his guilt. Nevertheless, win or lose, he always expressed his gratitude for my efforts and reckoned he owed me rather more than the pittance of a legal aid fee I received. And he said he would always be available to return the favour, if his help was ever needed. It was more than twenty years ago that I last acted for him. But, when I needed his help, I didn't have much difficulty tracking him down. And he still remembered his promise."

The cell door had been left open when Jenkins first entered, but Merryweather now went over and closed it. "I have already ascertained there are no visual or audio monitoring devices in this particular cell, Superintendent. But, before I say anything further, would you please be good enough to confirm that you, yourself, have not brought anything of that nature with you?"

Jenkins stretched out his arms slightly, in a gesture of openness. "No, I'm not wired, if that's what you're wondering. And I haven't even brought my notebook with me. But I should warn you that I have a good memory and that you're still under caution."

Sir Angus gave a gentle nod of understanding. "You may be interested to know that Snoopy Fairfax visited me here earlier this morning. He told me you were only on this case because of him. And that if you hadn't been, I'd probably still be a free man. He clearly thinks very highly of you."

"Did he also tell you the reason why he arranged for me to be on the case?" Jenkins asked.

Merryweather shook his head. "No, he didn't. And I didn't ask. I know Snoopy's a member of the British Intelligence community, so I suppose it's something very hush-hush. But he did tell me a few other things about you. For one thing, he told me that you're a particularly well educated police officer. You achieved a double first in Law at Cambridge, I understand. I imagine your education must have included studying a certain amount of history. I was wondering how this might have coloured and framed your particular view of the subject. Tell me, superintendent, do you see history as simply a list of facts to be remembered, or as a collection of lessons to be learned? Or, perhaps, you see it in some entirely different way?"

Jenkins again looked at his watch. He was becoming impatient. "I see it as something that is, sadly, all too often repeated. But can you please get to the reason you wanted to see me, Sir Angus. Today was to be my first day off in quite some time and I was hoping to spend at least some of it somewhere other than in a police cell."

Merryweather again gave a gentle nod. "I will, very soon, Superintendent, I promise. But please bear with me for just a few moments longer. I have only one last question to ask. Have you ever read any of Davey's published books or academic papers?"

"No," replied Jenkins emphatically.

"I thought not, so please let me try and enlighten you a little about the man's particular approach to his subject. I assure you it is relevant to the reason that you're here. You see, Davey viewed history in his own, rather unique way. To put it simply, he saw it as a plaything, something to be used for entertainment, primarily his own. Don't get me wrong, though, Davey was a brilliant man. In fact that was part of the problem. He has been at the centre of many great historical debates over the years. And he frequently came out on top. He's often been described by his contemporaries as a radical historian, but actually he was much more than that. To put it bluntly, superintendent, Davey was an iconoclast. He got his greatest satisfaction from ripping apart long held and generally accepted views and by denouncing a range of historical 'truths' as myths. He would, metaphorically speaking, quite happily tear down the house, before promptly moving on to carry out some further act of historical vandalism elsewhere. You might say, of course, that none of this really matters, because it's confined to the world of academia. While it remained like that I would agree with you. But I feared that Davey's scholarly mischief making was about to spill out into the real world."

"And what brought you to that conclusion?" Jenkins asked.

"It was because of the supposed 'hypothetical historical constitutional matter' that Davey raised with Smythe-Brightly," replied Merryweather. "Peregrine told me all about their conversation, when we had dinner together later on the same day. Since then he's informed me that he's also told you all about it. You see, Superintendent, Davey was not someone who wasted his time pondering over 'hypotheticals'. If he was giving his attention to some notion, however eccentric or outlandish it might appear to be, there had to be some very good reason for it. And I was keen to find out what it was. I knew that simply asking him about it would be pointless. He kept even his closest friends in the dark about what he was concerning himself with, right up until it was suddenly and unexpectedly launched into the public arena. That's why I decided to get hold of his research notebook. I'm quite familiar with the way he kept records. I knew that his methodology hadn't changed since we were undergraduates together, more than three decades ago."

"But why, exactly, were you so interested to find out what Davey was spending his time on?" Jenkins asked.

"Not to put too fine a point on it, Superintendent, I feared he could be on to something that might turn out to be profoundly disruptive and detrimental, to the peace and well being of the nation."

"That's quite a charge. I think you need to explain."

"And so I shall," responded Sir Angus, "starting with a bit of history. Ever since the time of the Restoration of the

Monarchy in 1660, there have been rumours that Charles II married in secret, at some time during his exile in France, and that a child was born to the marriage. Over the years, there have been numerous suggestions as to the identity of Charles's supposed bride, but, one by one, each of the claims has been debunked and exposed as very definitely false. Probably, the best known of these is Lucy Walters, mother of James, Duke of Monmouth, but that tale was shown to be a total fabrication a long time ago. However......."

Merryweather paused and took a sip of water before continuing.

".......however, there is one far less well known account that cannot be so easily invalidated. Shortly after William and Mary came to the throne in 1689, following the deposing of James II, a recently defrocked and excommunicated French Catholic priest, Aristide Bellange, arrived at the English Royal Court with an odd tale to tell. Bellange claimed that until his recent fall from grace he had been employed as an assistant to the Bishop's Archivist, in the Diocese of St Omer, in northwest France. He said that during his time there several volumes of records from a nearby parish, Bollezeelle, were brought to be deposited in the Archives, following the death of the incumbent priest, Father Levesque, who had served in the parish for the previous thirty years. Bellange explained that he had been given the job of reading through the deposited records, essentially to check on their completeness and legibility, before making a brief entry of their details in the Archives Register and then placing them in secure storage. He claimed it was whilst checking through these registers that he came across one especially striking entry that had been given particular prominence. It was the record of a marriage that took place in March 1659, between one Charles Stuart, identified in the entry only as a sojourner in the parish, and Marie de la Vallée, a local woman. The entry was followed in December of the same year by two more equally prominent entries, documenting the birth and baptism of a daughter, to parents Charles and Marie Stuart, and the subsequent death and burial of Marie, the wife of Charles Stuart."

The temperature in the enclosed space of the cramped police cell had risen noticeably since its door had been closed. It was beginning to feel quite stuffy. Merryweather again paused to take a sip of water. When he also removed his jacket, Jenkins noticed, for the first time, the gold cuff links he was wearing. Each of them was engraved with the same Chinese character, one identical to that which Jenkins remembered seeing engraved on Smythe-Brightly's signet ring and the same one that Professor Davey had so frequently handwritten in the margin of his copy of Mao's Little Red Book.

"Did Professor Davey give you those cuff links?" Jenkins asked.

"Yes, as a matter of fact he did. He gave them to me when I received my knighthood," replied Merryweather. "How did you manage to guess at that?"

"Professor Smythe-Brightly has a gold signet ring with the same Chinese character engraved on it," said Jenkins. "And he told me it was a gift from Professor Davey. Do you happen to know the meaning of the Chinese character?"

Merryweather gave a slight shrug. "I must say I've never given the matter much thought. But knowing Davey and his enthusiasm for Chinese mysticism, I'd guess it was, perhaps, symbolic of some particular quality or concept. Other than that I really couldn't say. I have no recollection of Davey ever offering an explanation. I'll carry on with my account now shall I?

Jenkins gave a gentle nod and Merryweather continued.

"Bellange considered the appearance of the name 'Charles Stuart' to be, of itself, something of an oddity in the register of the parish in question, especially since it had been written with such conspicuous extravagance. But what struck him even more, was the fact that Father Levesque had drawn in a small crown above the man's name, on each of the three occasions it appeared in the register. Levesque had also done the same above the names of the child and her deceased mother. Although very clearly unprincipled and corrupt, Bellange was an educated and intelligent man, and he quickly grasped the significance of what he'd come across. So, thinking these particular entries might one day prove profitable, he carefully removed the two relevant pages, before putting the Bollezeele parish registers into a sealed box and placing the box in one of the Archives' storage cupboards. Then, some years later, when he found himself in need of funds, after being defrocked and deprived of his ecclesiastical status, he decided to come to England, in the hope of selling the records to the new King and Queen."

"Bellange hadn't been defrocked for being a counterfeiter, by any chance, had he?" Jenkins enquired.

Merryweather gave a faint smile. "I can, of course, appreciate your scepticism, Superintendent, but the answer to your question is no. It seems that Bellange's wrong doings that led ultimately to his excommunication from the Catholic Church were of a rather more libidinous and carnal nature."

"So, was he successful with his pitch?" asked Jenkins. "Did he manage to sell the records to William and Mary?"

"Yes, so it would appear," replied Merryweather. "It seems he managed to persuade their Majesties of the validity of the documents and he was paid ten guineas for them."

"And how do you come to know all this?" asked Jenkins.

"Because a very detailed account of these events is documented in the Royal Archives, although in a section that is not open to anyone outside of a very tight circle. A circle of which I, as a senior legal adviser to the Court of St James, happen to be a member."

"Did Professor Davey also have access to these secret Royal Archives?" Jenkins enquired.

"Absolutely not," replied Merryweather. "And yet, the description he gave to Smythe-Brightly was a remarkably good fit. Anything he knew, he must have got from some other source. I wanted to find out what that source was and exactly what Davey did know. Of course it could all have been one very big coincidence, but I could only be sure of that, one way or the other, after reading the contents of his research notebook."

"If it's so highly confidential, why are you telling me?" Jenkins asked.

"A very good question," replied Merryweather. "It's mainly because I strongly suspect that you already know far more about this matter than you have so far revealed, including, I believe, being aware of the whereabouts of Davey's research notebook. And because Snoopy, someone whose judgement I trust on such matters, assures me that you are a man of the utmost integrity and, even more importantly, someone who can be trusted to keep a secret. Having said that, though, Snoopy has no idea what this particular secret is."

"Even if you're right and I do know where Professor Davey's research notebook is. I still haven't heard a good reason why I should tell you."

"Well, I haven't quite finished my explanation yet, Superintendent," responded Sir Angus. "You may recall that Davey asked Smythe-Brightly what he thought the constitutional position would be, if a direct descendant of the child born to Charles's clandestine marriage was alive today. And he was very clear about this supposed 'hypothetical' individual being a non-Catholic. Knowing Davey as I did, I believe he would not have posed that question unless he either knew, or at least was aware of strong evidence to suggest, that such an individual exists. Think what an opportunity for tearing down the house that would have presented him with. And, believe me, if he could, he would. Although Davey wrote extensively about Kings and Queens, he was, in fact, an ardent republican. Perhaps, even, on at least an emotional level, something of an anarchist. Maybe now you can appreciate my level of concern?"

"But Professor Davey is now dead, so why are you still concerned?" asked Jenkins.

"Because, although Davey is dead, his research notebook still exists," replied Sir Angus.

"So you want me to hand it over to you?"

"No, superintendent, you misunderstand. I want you to destroy it."

"I'll have to give that matter some thought," said Jenkins. "But you still haven't finished the story. For example, you never said what eventually happened to the two pages that were extracted from the Bollezeele parish records, after they were sold to William and Mary."

"The report in the Archives doesn't say. Perhaps they were destroyed," responded Merryweather. "They certainly haven't been retained within the Royal Archives."

"Or, perhaps, they're hidden away in a section of the Royal Archives that's even more secret than the one you've been allowed to see," suggested Jenkins. "But what about the defrocked French priest, Bellange? What happened to him?"

Merryweather gave a shrug. "I have no idea. There's no mention of him after he handed over the particular Bollezeele parish records. Perhaps he took his ten guineas and returned to France."

And, finally, what about King Charles' 'hypothetical' daughter? Has the record in the secret Archives very much to say about her?" Jenkins asked.

"No, not much at all," replied Merryweather. "Agents were sent to Bollezeele to make discreet enquiries, of course, but they returned to the English Royal Court with very little to show for their efforts. All they could report was that a female child had, indeed, been born into the de la Vallée household, at around the relevant time. But it seems she suddenly and mysteriously disappeared, to who-knows-where, in June 1680. It was assumed by the locals that she simply ran off to avoid the de la Vallée family creditors, of whom apparently there were many. The only other detail that's recorded in the Archives is the girl's name: Adeline."

Jenkins left Merryweather's police cell having already drawn at least one conclusion: Adeline's story, as recorded in Sir Bernard Harfield's first journal and related to him by Brazelle, was almost certainly true.

But he was rather puzzled by Merryweather's description of Professor Davey. Iconoclast and anarchist seemed extremely strong terms to use, especially when describing someone like Davey. After all, he was a wealthy and well connected Englishman, albeit colonially born. He was also a senior academic at one of the world's most prestigious universities. This seemed to Jenkins to be almost a textbook description of a member of the British Establishment. But, assuming Merryweather's portrayal of Davey was accurate, Jenkins wondered what could have caused him to think and behave in such an atypical and unpredictable way.

If Jenkins had probed a little more deeply into Davey's background he may well have found an answer to his question, and maybe one or two others in addition.

By 1975, Leonard Davey, Professor Davey's father, had risen to the rank of Assistant Commissioner in the Royal Hong Kong Police Force. It was also the year in which he was summarily dismissed from that Force, had his service pension entitlement cancelled, and was given a two year suspended prison sentence, following his conviction for corruption in public office. All this happened, despite his emphatic and consistent protestations of innocence, and the lack of any solidly tangible evidence against him. He had been found guilty, solely on the basis of unsubstantiated claims made by three more junior police officers who had, themselves, already been found guilty of corruption. They were also three officers who had in the past been disciplined by Assistant Commissioner Davey, and had lost rank and pay as a result.

This all occurred during a period when there was a major anti-corruption drive in the Crown Colony, one that affected all public services, especially the police. Perhaps because of the timing, and the Colony's Administration's desire to urgently restore the reputation of such an important service, especially one with the 'Royal' prefix in its name, standards of proof in such matters were occasionally lower than they might otherwise have been. But, whatever the reason, Leonard Davey considered he had been betrayed and made a scapegoat, by the very organisation to which he had given loyal and exemplary service for the best part of twenty years. The experience left him feeling vengeful towards the Establishment that had allowed, and perhaps even encouraged, it to happen.

It was a feeling which he either deliberately or unwittingly passed on to his adoring young son, Graham. Something that would, for ever afterwards, colour his son's world view.

It was an experience that would have crushed most men, but Leonard Davey was made of sterner stuff. Through hard work, determination and a degree of good fortune, he managed to carve out an entirely new career, one that very soon made him a wealthy man.

Leonard Davey's wife, however, did not cope so well. The ignominy of what happened to her husband overwhelmed her. She suffered a mental breakdown from which she never fully recovered. This was something else that had an impact on the development of the young Graham Davey.

DAY NINETEEN – SATURDAY

The success of the 2012 London Olympics served as an inspiration to many, not least to Iris Macbeth (nicknamed 'Lady', for the most obvious of reasons). But it wasn't sport that Iris was inspired to take up – it was a career in events management. At age eighteen, Iris dreamt that she too might one day be involved in the organisation and management of such a spectacular event.

Unfortunately, however, Iris's career did not go on to develop in quite the way that she hoped it would. Well over a decade later she was still waiting for her big break to arrive. So far, it had only been low budget and extremely parochial events that she'd been contracted to arrange and manage. Events such as kid's birthday parties, out-of-season coach trips for the retired and the occasional activity in the Prinsted Village Hall. It was true she'd once been commissioned to plan a wedding, but it was her sister's and she wasn't paid, so it didn't really count.

Iris felt she'd certainly given it her best shot and a major career change was beginning to look very much on the cards when, quite out of the blue, what looked like a golden opportunity suddenly and unexpectedly arrived. Iris received a phone call from Lady Frances Marshall, asking if she would organise a garden party for around three hundred guests. It was an event to be held in the grounds of Harfield House, Frances explained, and Iris would have less than six weeks in which to get it all planned and arranged. Given the relatively tight time frame, Iris knew it would be a challenge, but she was confident that it was one she could successfully meet. So, without a moment's hesitation, she accepted the commission.

Although Frances's approach was certainly unexpected, it hadn't exactly come from nowhere. As luck would have it, Iris's cousin, Layla, worked part-time as a maid at Harfield House. On hearing that Sir Damien and Lady Frances were proposing to hold a large garden party, Layla immediately put forward her cousin's name, as the ideal person to be commissioned to organise and manage the event. A few half truths had certainly been told in the way the suggestion was made, building up Iris's events management experience to rather more than it, in fact, amounted to. But Layla felt no guilt about this. She considered such exaggeration was pretty much the norm in business and, therefore, wholly legitimate.

It was exactly one year since Sir Damien and Lady Frances had returned from America, to once more take up residence at Harfield House, after an absence of almost two decades. By pure chance, it was a date that coincided with the couple's thirtieth wedding anniversary and they decided to mark this doubly noteworthy occasion. The event would also serve as a celebration of the recent engagement of Frances's half sister, Rose, to The Reverend Chris Brazelle.

When the day of the garden party finally arrived there was, in fact, even more to celebrate. Following her most recent head-to-toe medical examination, Rose had just been given a completely clean bill of health. In particular, her heart was confirmed as being in first class condition. It was a report that did not come as anything of a surprise to either

Frances, or to Rose herself, but it came as a great relief to Damien and Brazelle. And they both saw it as yet one more reason to crack open the Champagne.

For Iris Macbeth, on the other hand, the Harfield garden party would be the biggest and highest value event she had ever been commissioned to arrange. At least potentially, it would also be the most profitable. Much more importantly, though, Iris knew it presented her with an excellent opportunity to promote her business to a much wider and wealthier audience than she had ever done before. So it had to be a resounding success. Iris was determined that it would be.

In addition to many friends of the hosts, including Gerald and Jenny Caulfield, a significant number of Sir Damien's work colleagues and professional acquaintances, all drawn from the upper echelons of society, were also invited. So were the two dozen or so employees of the Harfield Estate, including Iris's cousin, Layla.

Superintendent Ifor Jenkins was also on the guest list and he took along with him DI Janet Kershaw as his plus-one. Kershaw was someone who neither Brazelle nor Rose had ever met before and as Jenkins was making the introductions, Rose noticed that Kershaw was barefoot.

"I don't normally walk around like this," explained Kershaw. "But, unfortunately, I've just managed to snap the heel off one of my shoes. It happened a few minutes ago when I was getting out of the car. So I had to choose between going barefoot or, walking with a limp."

"What shoe size are you?" asked Rose.

"Five," replied Kershaw.

"So am I," said Rose. "Come with me."

The two women went into the House, leaving Jenkins and Brazelle with the ideal opportunity to have a brief and very private conversation together. There were questions each wanted to ask the other, but without anyone else overhearing.

Jenkins was the only other person who knew that Brazelle was in possession of Professor Davey's research notebook, although he'd never actually seen it, let alone read what was in it. As the two men walked over to the bar in the marquee, he asked Brazelle what he now planned on doing with it.

The pair had discussed the matter briefly once before, when Jenkins called to let Brazelle know what Sir Angus Merryweather had told him during their meeting in his police cell. On that occasion they'd agreed that Davey's notebook should not be given to any third party. However, that was all that had so far been decided.

Since then, Brazelle had thought through a number of options. He'd even considered destroying the notebook, just as Sir Angus had requested. But he'd eventually rejected the idea. Instead, he'd hidden it away with the first of Sir Bernard's journals, the one in which Sir Bernard had recorded his great-grandmother's memoir.

He told Jenkins he'd placed them together in the basement strong room of the Harfield Estate Office, a building that had once been a bank, and a place he considered to be safe.

They were concealed amongst the countless number of other volumes, such as ledgers, log books, registers and goodness knows what else, that had been deposited down there. It was a collection that had been added to every now and again over the years, but had otherwise been left undisturbed. Brazelle could see no reason why that situation would change any time soon, if ever. In the meantime, if he ever felt the need to retrieve either of those two volumes, he knew exactly where they both were.

There were also a couple of questions to which Brazelle was hoping to get answers. For a start, what did Jenkins think was going to happen to Sir Angus Merryweather? His reputation and career were obviously in tatters. But was he likely to end up in jail?

"Sir Angus has only been charged with conspiracy to commit burglary," explained Jenkins. "The maximum sentence for that particular offence is fourteen years. Although, I doubt he'll get anything like that, nobody ever does, especially since he's already pleaded guilty to the offence. In fact, I wouldn't be surprised if he got away with just a suspended sentence, despite his refusal to tell the Court what his conspiracy with Charlie Rich was all about."

Given Sir Angus's refusal to publically explain the reasons for his actions there was, inevitably, a good deal of uninformed speculation as to what they might have been. Some of those suggested were really quite imaginative, fantastical even, but none came close to the truth. Apart from Sir Angus himself, Jenkins and Brazelle were the only other people who knew the true reason. And all three of them intended that it should, and would, remain that way.

Equally important, at least as far as Brazelle was concerned, was the question of whether or not Jenkins had finally accepted that Anna Popescu really was Sir Ted Gant's assassin, just as everyone else concerned with the case seemed to have done.

Jenkins gave a blunt response. "No I haven't, and I'm not sure I ever will. I still believe that Anna made the claim to cover for someone else, although I have no idea who. Anna knew she would be remembered as a murderer, because of killing Charlie Rich. So, if she owed Ted Gant's real assassin a favour, why not take the blame? After all, she had absolutely nothing more to lose. She knew she was never going to stand trial. But, you're right, I appear to be the only one who's been involved with the case who thinks that way. Everyone else seems convinced that Anna Popescu really was Gant's assassin, just as she claimed to be. Anyway, it doesn't really matter what I think, the investigation is now officially closed and everyone previously concerned with it, including me, has been reassigned to other cases. So, whether I agree or not, I guess that's the end of the matter, unless, of course, I ever come across a left-handed female with a motive for killing Gant, who also happens to be a crack-shot and has a fondness for expensive trainers."

It was all stuff that Brazelle didn't want to hear, but feared that he might. Ideally, he would have liked to have spent a little more time with Jenkins, so he could have another attempt at persuading him to change his mind and accept the situation, but there were other guests to greet and pay some attention to. Promising to catch up with him again later, Brazelle left Jenkins in the marquee to wait for Kershaw's return and went off to mingle elsewhere.

Because the engagement of her younger half-sister was one of the events being celebrated, Frances had gathered together a number of photos showing Rose at various stages of her life, and mounted them on a large board in the marquee. But it was far from being some random assortment of family snaps. Frances had put a great deal of thought into selecting which photographs of her sibling to include in the collection, before arranging and presenting them in chronological order.

Jenkins had been looking over the photographic display for several minutes when Frances noticed him and came over to say hello. "What do you think of the montage?" she asked.

"I think it's a fascinating biographical collection," replied Jenkins. "But I found one of the pictures, particularly intriguing. What's the story here?"

Jenkins pointed to a photograph showing Rose, at sometime in her late teens, holding aloft a trophy. Slung over her right shoulder was a rifle fitted with a telescopic sight. A taller and much older man, who was wearing a beaming smile and dressed in military fatigues, was standing by her side.

"It was taken at the State Fair seven years ago, when Rose was eighteen," explained Frances. "She'd just won the Annual Sharpshooter Competition. It was the second time she'd won it. Then she won it again the following year. Jerry, the man standing alongside her, is the one who taught her to shoot. He became one of Rose's martial arts teachers when she first took it up, aged thirteen. From the very start he said she was a natural, but then he spotted her potential with a rifle as well. He was ex-military and had served with the Green Berets as a sniper, so he knew what he was talking about. He took her hunting in the Appalachians a couple of times. And they never returned empty handed."

Frances wandered off, just as Janet Kershaw reappeared. She was no longer barefoot, but wearing a pair of training shoes. "Well, that was a stroke of luck," she said, "Rose being exactly the same shoe size as me. She gave me a more or less free choice from amongst the entire contents of her walk in shoe cupboard, which, by the way, appears to be slightly bigger than my entire bedroom. She must have at least a couple of hundred pairs of shoes and boots in there. And she seems to be particularly fond of Designer Brand trainers, just like the ones I'm wearing. God knows what they must have cost. I counted twenty three pairs altogether, including these."

As it got later in the day and the sun began to set, more and more of the guests thanked their hosts, said their goodbyes and departed. Eventually, only a couple of dozen people remained, including Jenkins and Kershaw. They were seated by the bar in the marquee, in deep conversation with Brazelle and Rose.

Prinsted was only fifteen miles from Oxford, the city in which DI Kershaw was born and bred, but her trip to Harfield House to attend the garden party, was the first time she had ever visited the place. This was all the more surprising since she had a family connection to the village. From at least the time of the English Civil War, right up to the late eighteenth century, several generations of her maternal grandmother's ancestors had lived there. When she mentioned this, Rose wondered aloud if they might possibly be related.

Kershaw was extremely doubtful. "I think that's highly unlikely. Your ancestors were the Lords and Ladies of the Manor and owned most of the Parish. But, from what my grandmother told me about her Prinsted ancestors, they were all labourers of one kind or another, and all as poor as church mice. Although there does seem to have been one exception."

"And who was that, exactly?" asked Rose.

"According to my grandmother he was the last of her ancestors to live here in Prinsted," explained Kershaw. "And he must have got some money from somewhere. Because, when he left Prinsted and moved to Oxford, sometime during the second half of the eighteenth century, he managed to buy a house there and start a business as a portrait artist and art dealer."

"That's quite a step up from being an impoverished labourer," commented Brazelle. "Like you say, he must have got some money from somewhere. Do you know very much about him, before he left Prinsted and moved to Oxford?"

"No, not much," Kershaw replied. "Although some years back my grandmother did tell me quite a bit about him, I'm afraid I've long since forgotten most of it. Apart from what I've just told you, all I can now remember is his name. And I can only remember that because it's quite an odd one. He was called Athanasius Sprout."

The sun had fully set, and as the last few stragglers moved out of the marquee, Iris Macbeth arrived to oversee the clearing up. The day had been a great success. And she knew it. Frances had allowed her to mount a small promotional sign at one end of the bar, together with a box of her business cards, and she was pleased to see that most of them had been taken by guests. What might follow from that, only time would tell.

Brazelle and Rose led Jenkins and Kershaw through the House and towards the front door. When they got to the entrance hall Kershaw began to take off the trainers she was wearing, intending to give them back to Rose.

"Keep them for now," said Rose. "You can't go home barefoot or walking with a limp." She then picked up a sheet of notepaper and a pen from the hall table, wrote down her phone number and handed it to Kershaw. "Give me a call when you've got some free time and we can arrange to have lunch together," she said. "You can return the trainers then."

It was a proposition that clearly appealed to Kershaw. She left Harfield House not only feeling that she'd had a really great day, but also that she'd made a new friend.

Jenkins, on the other hand, was left rather conflicted, confused even. He'd known from the very beginning, that Rose was someone with a very strong motive for wanting vengeance against Sir Ted Gant, the man who had ordered the murder of her father, Sir Cornelius, when she was only five years old. But it was only earlier that day he'd discovered she was a highly skilled sharpshooter with a fondness for expensive trainers. And now, as she wrote down her phone number to give to Janet Kershaw, he noticed something else of which he'd previously been unaware – Rose was left-handed.

As he drove away from Harfield House, Jenkins tried to convince himself that this was all, surely, just a matter of coincidence.

But, of course, it wasn't.

DAY TWENTYSIX – SATURDAY

Since experiencing his recent tour of the interior of James Caulfield's newly renovated cottage, Brazelle had changed his mind about creating a single painting of just its exterior. Instead, equally inspired by some of Van Gogh's sketches he'd recently seen, he decided to create two drawings using just pen and ink. One was a finely detailed image of the cottage's restored seventeenth century bedroom, whilst the other was a line drawing of the cottage itself. Once completed, he took both pictures to show Caulfield and invited him to select one of them to keep as a gift.

Equally impressed by both of Brazelle's creations, Caulfield found choosing between the two of them difficult. But he eventually opted for the drawing of the restored bedroom. After having it framed, he said he would hang it on the wall in the dining room, in place of the missing parchment that Professor Davey had taken away, but never returned. He had given up all hope of ever seeing it again.

Some changes had been made in the dining room since Brazelle last visited. For one thing, the portrait of a woman now hung on the wall directly opposite the parchments. It was a painting Brazelle had never seen before and, as he followed Caulfield into the dining room, his eyes were instantly drawn to it. For a few moments he appeared transfixed, but it certainly wasn't the quality of the artwork that fascinated him. At best, that could only be described as mediocre. It was realising the woman had been painted wearing Queen Henrietta Maria's rubies, that left him momentarily speechless. Although hard for him to believe, Brazelle had absolutely no doubt about it: the jewellery worn by the woman in the portrait was identical to that which appeared in the portraits of both Adeline and Justine. But how could this be?

Caulfield followed Brazelle's gaze. "I put it up there only yesterday," he said. "So you're the very first person to see it. I'd almost forgotten I had it, but then I stumbled across it whilst sorting through some old storage boxes I'd put up in the attic years ago. I know it's not a particularly fine painting, but it's the only old family portrait I've got. And there's a bit of history attached to it as well. If nothing else, I thought it might make a good conversation piece, just like the old parchments in here."

Brazelle was curious to know who the woman in the portrait was.

"Her name is Lucy de Calvairac," Caulfield explained. "She was the only daughter of my five times great grandfather, Isaac. I believe that makes her my five times great aunt."

"Do you know very much about her?" asked Brazelle.

"I've never actually seen any written records that have anything to say about her," replied Caulfield, "but some information has been orally transmitted down through the generations. How much of it is true, though, I have no idea. But still, that's not a requirement of claimed family history, is it? It doesn't have to be true, just so long as it's interesting. Even better if it's scandalous."

"And was it scandalous in Lucy de Calvairac's case?" asked Brazelle.

"That depends on your point of view," replied Caulfield. "I'd say it was sad, rather more than scandalous. According to what I've been told, she never married, lived a fairly uneventful life and then, at the age of forty two, she hanged herself. Apparently, she did it just a few days after that portrait was completed."

"You'd never guess she was feeling suicidal from how she appears in her portrait. She's got a look of relaxed contentment," observed Brazelle. "Do you know what caused her to take her own life?"

"It was a case of unrequited love, or so the story goes," said Caulfield.

The level of skill displayed by the painter of Lucy's portrait was, in Brazelle's opinion, at best modest. And he also judged it to be, in some respects, quite inconsistent. It seemed to him, that significantly more care and effort had gone into painting the jewellery that Lucy was wearing, than into painting Lucy herself. To Brazelle this suggested that the painter's imagination had been captured rather more by Queen Henrietta Maria's rubies, than by the appearance or personality of his subject.

As far as Brazelle was aware, James Caulfield had never seen the recently discovered portrait of Adeline. Was it possible that James Caulfield knew about Queen Henrietta Maria's rubies and their connection to the Harfield family? Brazelle was keen to find out. "Do you know anything about the jewellery that Lucy's wearing in her portrait?" he asked.

"Not very much, no, beyond the fact that the stones appear to be rubies, symbols of love, health and wisdom, I understand," said Caulfield. "And although I'm no expert in such matters, I imagine the jewellery was quite valuable. From what

I remember being told, it was supposedly bequeathed to Lucy by some wealthy old lady in her Will. But the woman's identity has long since been forgotten."

"By the sound of it, what happened to the rubies has also been forgotten," said Brazelle.

"That's right," confirmed Caulfield. "The jewellery went missing many years ago. Apparently, it disappeared around the time Lucy killed herself. Perhaps she gave it away, after deciding to take her own life. Or maybe it was stolen. I believe suspicion did fall on one individual at the time, but nothing was ever proved. Oddly enough, the suspect was none other than the artist who painted her portrait. And it's claimed he was also the subject of her unrequited passion. But how much, if any, of that particular tale is true, I really have no idea."

Brazelle moved forward to read the tiny writing in the bottom right of Lucy's portrait: *'19th July 1770 Athanasius Sprout'*

Now that really was a coincidence.

THE LAST WORD

A few weeks passed and much had changed.

Brazelle had resigned himself to the fact that documentary support for Adeline's alleged claim would, most probably, never be found. But even if it was, what did it matter? Any legitimate claim to the English Throne the Harfield family may once have had, disappeared with the death of Sir Cornelius.

Following his recent marriage to Rose, Brazelle had moved into Harfield House, and his temporary appointment as Prinsted's parish priest had been made permanent. After the birth of Gerald and Jenny Caulfield's first child, a daughter christened Esther, Jenny had decided that motherhood was a far more compelling vocation than the priesthood. Consequently, she had resigned from her position as Prinsted parish priest, allowing the role to pass to Brazelle, her erstwhile temporary replacement.

In recognition of his successfully applied efforts in the Charlie Rich case, Jenkins had received yet another commendation, although this time without an accompanying promotion. And he had made a permanent transfer to Thames Valley Police from the Met, whilst retaining his senior rank. Amongst other things, this made it much easier for him and DI Kershaw, who had also received a commendation, to continue developing their out-of-hours relationship.

The Davey and Gant investigations were now both officially closed. As far as the legal authorities were concerned, all miscreants involved in those two cases, were now either dead or had been arrested, tried in a court of law and appropriately sentenced. Only Jenkins, it seemed, still retained any doubts about the truthfulness of Anna Popescu's claim to have been Sir Ted Gant's assassin. But what could he do about it? If he raised any alternative theory, he knew he would have to swim against the raging tide of received wisdom, a pursuit that rarely ends well.

And what of the mysterious Chinese character that Jenkins had found so intriguing? The one Professor Davey had written alongside so many of the 267 aphorisms in Mao's Little Red Book and the same one that was engraved on Sir Peregrine Smythe-Brightly's gold signet ring and, on the cuff links belonging to Sir Angus Merryweather. Gifts presented to them by Professor Davey at the time each received his knighthood. A solution to this puzzle was eventually found.

On one of his ever more frequent visits to The Celestial Gardens Chinese Bar and Restaurant, Jenkins showed to Jason, the Chinese barman, the copy of the Chinese character he had drawn in his notebook and asked if he could tell him what it meant.

Jason looked rather surprised. "Are you sure you drew it correctly?" he asked.

"Yes, I'm quite confident that it's a pretty good copy of what I saw," replied Jenkins. "Is there a problem?"

"No, there isn't a problem," replied Jason. "It's just that you've drawn the Chinese character for goushi. And in English goushi means shit."

Milton Keynes UK
Ingram Content Group UK Ltd.
UKHW021321281024
2424UKWH00003B/3